MW01131662

Cowboys for Christmas

Cowboys Online, Volume 1

Jan Springer

Published by Jan Springer, 2014.

Also by Jan Springer

Cowboys Online
Cowboys for Christmas
Cowboys In Her Pocket
Loving Her Cowboys

Kidnap Fantasies
Jade's Fantasy
Zero To Sexy
Christmas Lovers

Pleasure Bound
A Hero's Welcome
A Hero Escapes
A Hero Betrayed
A Hero's Kiss
A Hero Wanted
Captive Heroes

Pleasure Bound Boxed Set
Pleasure Bound : COMPLETE SERIES SciFi Erotic Romance
Boxed Set

Tentacles Shifter Erotic Romance
Taken by Him

The Key Club
A Merry Menage Christmas
Sophie's Menage
Jewel's Menage
Jaxie's Menage

A Homecoming Menage Christmas

The Outlaw Lovers
Jude
The Claiming
Colter's Revenge
Tyler's Woman
Resistance
The Outlaw Lovers

Standalone
A Touch of Menage Boxed Set
Shades of Menage Boxed Set
Naughty Girl Desires Boxed Set
Nice Girl Naughty
Sinderella Sexy
The Biker and The Bride
The Fire Within
Bared to Him
Pleasure Bound : A Futuristic Adult Romance Boxed Set
Merry Menage Kisses Boxed Set
Inner Girl Rising
Stripped Naked
Risqué Girl Delights Boxed Set
A Holiday Menage
Ménage À Trois

Watch for more at www.janspringer.com.

Cowboys for Christmas

Jan Springer

Jennifer Jane (JJ) Watson has spent the past ten Christmases in a maximum-security prison.

The last thing she expects is to get early parole, along with a job on a remote Canadian cattle ranch serving Christmas holiday dinners to three of the sexiest cowboys she's ever met!

Rafe, Brady and Dan thought they were getting a couple of male ex-cons to help out around their secluded ranch, but instead they get an attractive and very appealing female.

In the snowbound wilds of Northern Ontario, female companionship is rare.

It's a good thing the three men like to share...

They're dominating, sexy-as-sin and they fill JJ with the hottest ménage fantasies she's ever had. Suddenly she's craving cowboys for Christmas and wishing for something she knows she can never have...a happily ever after.

Cowboys for Christmas
Cowboys Online Book 1
Published by Spunky Girl Publishing
Copyright 2014 by Jan Springer
Discover other titles by Jan Springer at
http:www.janspringer.com
Cover Art by Talina Perkins, Bookin It Designs
Edited by Julie Naughton

Notes

Chapter One

"Yeah, perfect. Thanks for the favor, Jenna. We appreciate it. She'll be there sometime tonight."

Jennifer Jane Watson stared at her parole officer, Sabrina Heathers, as she spoke on the phone. The officer kept glancing at JJ with an encouraging smile and a hopefulness that JJ just didn't feel. Actually, she hadn't had an ounce of hope inside her since the day the jury had said she was guilty more than ten years ago on her eighteenth birthday.

It didn't matter that JJ had killed her stepfather in self-defense. Or that she'd killed him because he'd just beaten her mother to death. Nope, the jury decided she was guilty of premeditated murder because she'd taken the law into her own hands and dished out the justice herself.

They'd been wrong in convicting her. Hell, mistakes were made every day in the judicial system, and she'd had to learn to live with that knowledge or go insane.

"I just confirmed the perfect job for you. All the proper channels are in agreement, so it's a go," Sabrina said as she hung up the phone. She grabbed a pad of paper and began writing.

Yeah, like JJ wanted a job. She'd just been locked up in a six-by-eight foot prison cell for, like, ever. The last thing she wanted to be was a drone and get stuck on some crummy assembly line or doing some nine-to-five receptionist job. No, she wanted her freedom. She wanted to do her own thing and pretend the last ten years had never happened.

JJ gazed around the parole officer's tiny cluttered office and frowned at the small artificial Christmas tree set upon the filing cabinet. It looked dreary with plastic ornaments and artificial tinsel. Just like her elderly parole officer looked bogus with her long black false eyelashes, her ultra-long red fingernails that had to be phony, and her bleached-blonde hair pulled tight off her face to prevent her wrinkles from showing.

No, she didn't want any more of this dull atmosphere. She wanted a natural live tree, like the ones they'd had when she'd been a kid. She wanted to smell pine trees and string popcorn and hang fragile glass ornaments on the tree and watch pretty colorful lights flicker at windows of houses.

"Correctional Services partakes in many different programs and participates with many employers who are willing to hire recently paroled cons. You were lucky you applied for the pilot Freedom Run project so you could get early and full parole. Lucky, too, that I know Jenna personally. She's the owner of Cowboys Online and Jenna has been placing people from the prison system through her company for years. Let's hope your lucky streak continues."

Yeah, lucky. Not.

Sabrina paused. If she was waiting for JJ to kiss her ass and say thank you, she'd be waiting until next year.

JJ resisted the impulse to flick Sabrina the middle finger and tell her she didn't want any favors. She wanted her freedom. But she kept her mouth shut, like the way she'd been trained. The last thing she wanted was to get tossed back behind bars. She'd suck up Sabrina's crap and when she had the chance, she'd make herself disappear.

Her parole officer smiled and for a split second JJ almost warmed to the woman. Maybe she was being sincere? Maybe she really did care about what happened to her? But she clamped down on the warm fuzzy feeling. No, she didn't want to be chummy with anyone in the judicial system.

"You'll be working on a cattle ranch."

A cattle ranch? JJ blinked in surprise. That sounded promising. She liked animals and she loved the outdoors.

"It's not just any cattle ranch. This one deals in organic beef cattle and is situated in Northern Ontario. In the wilderness. Nothing but you, an elderly female role model who used to be a con, your bosses, wild cattle and thousands of acres of forests and meadows.

The Ontario wilderness? She could disappear over there.

"Your free spirit will love it."

Yeah, right. Like Sabrina knew her? Sure, they'd been meeting over the last few months to figure out a release plan. Sabrina as well as JJ's psychologist and the corrections officers had said nice things about her at the parole hearing, but everybody's cheeriness and optimism only irritated JJ.

"This position just came up through the Freedom Run program. They need an assistant to the elderly female cook & housekeeper and you'll be available for other odd jobs as they come up, such as a cook on cattle drives."

She would be a freaking housekeeper and cook? As if she knew anything about either. Those kinds of jobs were so not her.

"There is only one little problem," her parole officer said.

Sabrina's red lips dipped into a frown and JJ's tummy did a not-so-nice roll.

As if I don't have enough problems?

"As I mentioned, the ranch is in a very secluded area. So the only way in is by private plane. I have your flying schedule here." She ripped a sheet off her pad of paper and slid it across her desk for JJ to take a look at.

JJ didn't make a move for it. The word plane reverberated around in her mind. There was no way she could get onto a plane.

Anxiety swelled inside her chest. Suddenly the walls began to waver and then move in around her. She grabbed the edges of her chair and held on as a wave of dizziness swept over her. Was it suddenly getting hard to breathe? Yes, it was getting hard to breathe. She was going to suffocate!

"I realize you've been having a problem with claustrophobia, anxiety and panic attacks. So I've put in an order for a prescription for appropriate meds to keep you calm during the trip. You'll be fine if you take them."

Oh crap. I am so not getting onto any plane. I'd rather go back to prison.

"The ranch is called Moose Ranch and it's run by three men around your age. They've agreed to allow you to work there on a conditional basis. If things go well, they will hire you on a contract basis. You'll get paid monthly. You'll have to check in with me two times a week for the first month, once a week for another month and then once a month thereafter. And I may do unexpected spot checks too."

The woman leaned closer and her blue gaze turned intense and her look was stern.

Despite not wanting to be intimidated by the officer, JJ shivered.

"JJ, I don't have to tell you how lucky you are to get an early parole with the Freedom Run program. You only got it because of an overcrowding problem and due to your record for not getting into trouble. If this job doesn't work out, you'll be sent back to prison and I don't have to tell you that your next chance to get out won't come until your next parole hearing, and that won't be for a long time. Do you understand my meaning?"

"I understand," JJ managed to say between frantic gasps for air. A familiar nausea, compliments of a panic attack, churned her tummy.

The officer smiled, seemingly satisfied that she'd managed to ruin JJ's day with the talk about a plane.

"Good. Good. I'll call the guard in and she can get you set up. Any questions?"

JJ's grip on the chair tightened as the walls began to crush her.

"Yeah, where's the nearest bathroom? I need to puke."

Parole officer Sabrina Heathers listened to the convict retching in the adjoining office bathroom and shook her head in disappointment. At the mention of flying, she'd read the panic flare in JJ's brown eyes. She'd wished the notes she'd read by JJ's prison psychologist had been overstated. She'd naively hoped that JJ's anxiety problems could be overcome if JJ knew she was getting out of prison. Maybe she'd been wrong?

She had no idea why she'd taken it upon herself to make it as easy as possible for JJ on the outside with a good job. It had helped that the woman who ran Cowboys Online had a government contract with the Correctional Service of Canada. Jenna was a friend of hers from her high school days, and Sabrina also knew the three men who owned the Moose Ranch.

They were good, hard-working, decent men and she had the feeling they would like JJ. She just hoped that they didn't regret taking her, especially with her anxiety issues.

Another loud retch sprang from the bathroom and echoed through Sabrina's office. She grimaced at the violent sound. If the mere mention of a plane made the woman lose it, she had to wonder how long JJ would last out there in the wilds and seclusion of Northern Ontario.

"Did you get the cattle secured in the barn?" Brady called out when he heard Dan and Rafe stomp into the nearby mudroom located beside the ranch office.

"All settled in. It's going to be a cold night tonight. The snow storm is coming too. Black clouds to the north," Rafe shouted back.

Brady frowned and lifted his gaze from the bookkeeping records and peered out the office window that was right in front of his desk. It was four o'clock and getting dark fast. The sun had dipped behind the pine trees spreading black shadows everywhere. From here, he could barely see the ice-covered lake where the plane was going to land. The large lake had been frozen for a good two months and would hold up with no problem beneath the weight of the plane.

They'd been lucky this year. It was already late November and not much snow so far. But it appeared as if that was about to change. Rafe was right. Dark clouds loomed on the horizon.

The plane bringing their new employee and their supplies was a little over an hour late and coming in from the north. He hoped they hadn't been caught in the snowstorm. He'd give the plane another five minutes and then he'd get on the satellite phone and send out an alert.

Dan, the youngest partner in their cattle venture, suddenly opened the office door and popped his head into the office. A whisper of cold air blew against the back of Brady's neck, making him shiver. He wanted to yell at Dan to shut the freaking door as he was letting all the hot air out, when movement out the window and in the sky caught his attention. A small red plane swooped in over the tree line and angled toward the lake.

"They're here," Dan said. He left and then Brady could hear the drone of the plane's engines.

Red plane. That would mean Kelly was flying in. He liked Kelly. She was a pretty blonde with cheerful blue eyes and was a few years younger than he. She worked for North Country Air, a bush-flying business located a few hundred miles to the north of Moose Ranch.

He'd heard rumors that she was in the air more than she was on land. He'd asked her out a couple of times, but she'd politely declined, giving an excuse that she didn't date. He wondered if she ever would date again after the horrific way she'd lost her smokejumper fiancé a couple of years ago in a raging forest fire. His body had never been found.

"Let's go out and greet them," Brady said a moment later, when he joined them in the mudroom. He grabbed his jacket.

Rafe and Dan grimaced and didn't move to put their winter gear back on.

"Come on, let's get a move on. Kelly is going to need help unloading the supplies and I can't get the snowmobile down in time," Brady prodded as he pulled on his black hat.

Rafe shook his head. "Sorry, but I have a cold ass that needs warming."

"Yeah, and my belly is screaming for food," Dan said quickly as he hurriedly tugged off his boots and gazed up at Brady from the bench seat. "You know I won't be able to get dinner on the table if I'm out there greeting some old convict."

Rafe chimed in. "Yeah, you can thank Mrs. Wilson for skipping out on us without notice."

"Wasn't her fault she couldn't take another winter here," Brady said.

He'd felt sorry for the sixty-five year old ex-con who'd been working for them for a couple of years. She'd finally confided in them that she couldn't handle the desolation any more, let alone another long freezing winter. She'd left unexpectedly just last week, secretly calling in one of the bush pilots over at North Country Air to get her out of here. Thankfully, his sister, Jenna, had answered his call for help and was sending a replacement through her Cowboys Online service.

A sharp slap to Brady's back made him wince.

"Besides," Rafe said. "You've been warming your ass off in here all day. We've done your share of the work out in the cold. Now it's your turn outside and getting some fresh air."

"Yeah, maybe you can ask Kelly out again," Dan said.

"Then she can turn you down again," Rafe chuckled.

He winked as he and Dan rushed past him out of the mudroom and into the main house.

Irritation bristled through Brady. No way was he asking Kelly out again. A man could only take rejection for so long before he got the message loud and clear. She wasn't ready, and he wasn't her type.

"Fine. But I expect dinner to be ready when we get back!" he shouted.

"Yeah, yeah, yeah," Dan called back.

The drone of the airplane grew lower as Brady slipped on his boots. Kelly had probably already landed and was wondering why no one was there to help her with their supplies and to greet the new guy.

He opened the mudroom door and gasped as the bitter wind blasted against his face. He shivered and snuggled his chin deep into his jacket, then began to jog along the path toward the lake, a quarter of a mile down the low sloping hill.

Sometimes he wondered what the heck he'd been thinking coming up north to carve out a cattle empire in the middle of a desolate wilderness. He should have stayed in Toronto where he'd had a nice cushy corner office and played estate lawyer. But he'd become bored with his job and had begun to crave adventure.

Brady frowned as he spied Kelly hopping out of her plane with a couple of suitcases and added it to the several crates she'd already piled on the lake. Her blonde hair glistened in the twilight and when she spied him approaching, she waved. Then she stepped back into her plane.

A moment later, she appeared with another person. Shadows had wrapped around the plane and he found it difficult to make out the features of the newcomer, but he was already disappointed in the man's small size. The person was no bigger than Kelly and he was wrapped head to toe in winter gear as if he were terrified of the cold.

Great. Just great.

The person was dwarfed in a heavy green winter jacket with a fur-lined hood pulled over his head. A red scarf covered his face. They'd been expecting someone with muscles. Someone who could help them on the cattle drives, pitch in with some heavy chores and assist with the cooking and housekeeping.

This person was already sitting down on their suitcases, instead of carrying them toward the ranch house.

"Hiya Brady. Got your cargo!" she called out as he approached. "Wish I could stay, but I need to scoot. Storm is coming in and I need to leave now or I'll be staying here for awhile. Not that I wouldn't mind, but I have contracts to fill and can't afford to get stranded down this way."

He still hadn't reached her, so he yelled a thanks and a threw her a wave. She waved back, turned and climbed into her plane and settled into the cockpit. A moment later, she was roaring her plane over the smooth ice.

By the time he reached the lake and the new recruit, Kelly's plane was disappearing over the tree line and the smell of booze was prevalent in the air.

Are you fucking kidding me? The new employee is drunk?

The sound of a hiccup made him curse.

Shit! He could not tolerate a drunk. Not on his ranch.

"Oh, you look so grumpy," a sweet feminine voice said.

Brady blinked as shock reverberated through him.

A woman?

"Grumpy, but cute." Her words were followed by another hiccup.

As she raised her head to look at him, he spied velvety brown hair tumbling from beneath her scarf. She had a luscious-looking mouth, a pert nose, and the longest eyelashes he'd ever seen.

She smiled up at him and he caught dimples popping in both her cheeks. Dimples that made him feel as if he'd just been sucker punched, but in a really nice way.

"Plane rides make me so nervous and I...b-broke into Kelly's b-booze and self-medicated. She was so p-pissed when she found out." She laughed prettily. The sound was like a gentle twinkle and made his heart skip a beat.

Holy shit. Why was he even reacting to her? She was all wrong for the job. All wrong for this place. Everything was suddenly just totally out of whack.

"Table is all set. I even lit a couple of candles to make the new guy feel more comfortable. How's the stew?" Rafe asked as he strolled over to where Dan stood stirring the food in his huge Crock-pot.

"All ready," Dan said as he withdrew a long wood spoon, placed it on a plate, then removed the apron. He moved over to allow Rafe a peek.

Rafe's mouth watered at the succulent, tangy smell.

"Impressive," he replied. He meant it too.

Tomato sauce bubbled in the pot and he caught glimpses of sage, oregano, onions and potatoes mixed with generous chunks of meat. His stomach picked that moment to growl. He was surprised Dan could cook so well.

"I do declare if that isn't the best compliment you've ever given me," Dan said in a feminine voice and batted his eyelashes at Rafe.

"Screw off," he rolled his eyes and shook his head. Sometimes Dan could be funny, but not now. Not when he could eat a freaking bear. That's exactly what was in the pot. Black bear meat. One of his favorites. The meal had been simmering the entire day.

Aside from the bear, the other ingredients had been homegrown in the garden Dan had created at the back of the ranch house. He grew everything in cages so the animals couldn't get to it and he had to admit, homegrown was a hell of a lot better tasting than the store-bought stuff they ordered in through North Country Air.

"You two. Get your asses down to the lake and pick up the shit that Kelly brought in," Rafe's gruff and very irritated voice shot through the kitchen like a missile.

Rafe whirled around to find Brady standing in the hallway. The newcomer stood right beside him and appeared...tipsy?

"What the fuck?" Dan's question was drowned by a furious look from Brady.

Uh oh.

Brady was really pissed and the instant Rafe saw the new recruit's face, he knew why. They'd asked for two strong men who knew how to cook and clean, as well as someone who could assist the cook in the kitchen and them doing chores. Instead, a young woman stood in front of them.

"A mistake?" Rafe asked as he studied the woman. She was pretty. She had a light spattering of freckles across her flushed cheeks. Her face was pale and she had an odd smile flirting with the edges of her lips as she stared at them with big brown eyes that reminded him of an innocent doe.

"A big one," Brady acknowledged.

"Oh, two more cuties." She placed her mittened hand over her mouth hiccupped, her eyes twinkling with amusement.

Brady raised his eyebrows and frowned at her. He then quickly focused his attention back to Dan and himself.

"Get the stuff off the lake before the bears get a whiff and we lose our food supply," Brady growled.

Dan swore softly again.

Rafe couldn't stop himself from grinning. A pretty lady instead of two strong men. How wrong could Jenna get their instructions? This was an interesting turn of events.

"I think it's best if we leave these two alone," Dan said and winked at Rafe. He wanted to warn Dan that this was not the time to piss off an already-pissed-off Brady, but Dan was moving past the duo and heading to the mudroom.

"Maybe some coffee is in order? Want me to get it started?" Rafe asked, wanting to stay indoors and near this lady. Suddenly he wanted to know everything about her.

"I'll take care of it," Brady growled.

Rafe nodded and forced himself to rip his gaze from the pretty woman. As he was about to pass Brady and the woman who continued smiling, Brady stopped him with a stern look.

"When you're done helping Dan, get Jenna on the satellite phone. She's got a lot of explaining to do."

Chapter Two

"A woman?" Dan grumbled as he followed Rafe along the trail toward the shed where they kept their snowmobiles.

Dan just couldn't believe their new employee was a woman, especially when they'd specifically asked for two men. After Mrs. Wilson's unexpected departure, they'd resigned themselves to thinking women just wouldn't like it out here. They'd contacted Jenna, asking her for replacements.

"Unless your eyes are playing tricks on you too, it's a woman," Rafe replied as he opened the shed door. His voice sounded somber. Heck, Dan was feeling pretty low himself. This cattle ranch was no place for a female.

As Mrs. Wilson had pointed out, there were no shopping centers around. No grocery stores. No regular female companionships unless you counted the women bush pilots who worked for North Country Air, but they only dropped by about once a month to deliver the supplies that Moose Ranch ordered online.

They stepped inside the shed and Dan flipped the light switch. The fluorescent lamps flickered on and illuminated the contents. Three yellow snowmobiles, sleds and trailers were parked in such a way as someone just needed to hitch up a trailer or sled, hop onto the machine, pop the key into the ignition and ride out of here.

Dan grabbed the key for the closest snowmobile and tossed Rafe the key. He hitched the sled and Dan opened the shed doors and quickly climbed onto the seat behind Rafe.

"We tried like hell to entertain Mrs. Wilson," Rafe continued as he tugged his hood up over his hat, then put on his goggles.

"And she still left us. The last thing we need is to take care of another woman with all the work that we have to do around here."

Dan followed Rafe's lead and pulled his hood over his toque, and put on his goggles. Despite the short ride down to the lake, it would be colder than if they walked, but the trip would be quicker with the snow machine.

"Don't let this female hear you say that. She strikes me as the feminist type," Rafe said.

"What gives you that idea?"

Rafe fell silent for a moment, then continued in a puzzled voice.

"Why else would Jenna send her here? She probably thinks this chick is tough as nails. Hell, we thought Mrs. Wilson was stronger than an ox, but we were wrong. Unless Jenna made a mistake in sending that lady here?"

"Maybe," Dan acknowledged. He doubted it.

He'd known Jenna for as long as he'd known Brady and the rest of their siblings. If anything, she was as meticulous as Brady. If she'd made a mistake, she would have corrected it already and not sent this woman.

Dan shook his head and grabbed hold of Rafe's waist as the snowmobile roared to life. He suspected Jenna knew exactly what she was doing and he wasn't necessarily sure it was a good thing.

JJ felt great. For one thing, she was off that horridly small plane that had droned on endlessly. She was now tucked away in a log ranch house. When she'd sat on her suitcases on that frozen lakes and saw the buttery wash of lights splashing from the windows of the sprawling log house, and saw the gray spiral of smoke from one of the stone chimneys, her heart had clutched with the feeling of coming home.

Several outbuildings were spread haphazardly all around the house and she'd spied several cattle in corrals as she'd walked up the trail past the barn.

Now she had a hot-looking guy pouring her a mug of steaming black coffee while she sat at an awesomely long pine table that looked like something right out of the old western John Wayne movies she loved watching on the small black-and-white TV she'd had in her cell.

Fortunately, the pills she'd been prescribed and had popped into her mouth back in Quebec had prevented her from going into full panic mode on the way to the airport. Sabrina had accompanied her onto a small plane, which had taken them to some isolated airport in Northern Ontario. The plane ride hadn't been as bad as she'd thought. But then she'd been dropped off at a tiny airport with one small building and nothing but snow and trees surrounding a single runway with several very small bush planes parked here and there, that familiar claustrophobia she'd experienced in Sabrina's office had begun to claw through her.

Another pill later, she said goodbye to Sabrina and reluctantly climbed into that tin coffin of a red plane that belonged to Kelly. Before she'd been able to fly into a full-blown panic attack and jump out of the plane in mid-air, she'd spied the case of red wine that the sweet pilot had been carrying just behind JJ's seat.

By the time Kelly had caught on that JJ was drinking, she was piss-drunk and two sheets to the wind and really didn't give a shit if the plane crashed or if the walls squeezed her to death.

Now she was being blessed with such a hunky cowboy that she wondered if she'd fallen into a drug- and alcohol-induced dream. She frowned as she gazed up at him. He wore a scowl on his luscious lips. Lips that she wouldn't mind kissing. And his eyes were bluer than the sky she'd flown through.

"Something's missing about you." She tried to figure out exactly what that might be.

"The only thing missing about me is my common sense," he muttered.

He pushed the mug closer to her. He still wore his winter clothing and so did she, but the icy wind had put a chill into her bones and she wasn't quite warm yet. He appeared to be getting hot, because suddenly he was chucking his coat and settling it on the back of one of the chairs. He wore a red-and-black hunter fleece jacket and a black turtleneck. He tore his black wool hat off his head and set it on the table. That's when it hit her.

"Now I know what's missing. Your cowboy hat. I was told there would be sexy cowboys out here."

Had she just said the word sexy? She hiccupped. Oh, who cared. He looked hot. He was well over six feet, just like the other two men she'd seen earlier. He had broad shoulders and a strong jaw shadowed with dark bristle. His hair was dark brown and wavy, medium length and a bit scruffy. He needed a haircut, but those dreamy blue eyes...

"Cowboy hats turn me on. Put yours on. " She hiccupped.

Oops, she'd just revealed one of her secrets to him.

He rolled his eyes as if he were self-conscious and his face appeared so red. Was he embarrassed?

"A shy cowboy. So sexy." She hiccupped. Oops, she'd just said that sexy word again.

"If I put on my cowboy hat, you'll drink your coffee?" His scowl turned to one of hopefulness. Gosh, who was she to dash hopes?

"Sure. I'll do anything for a man wearing snug jeans, tons of muscles and a cowboy hat."

He stood so fast his chair toppled over behind him. He swore and swooped it back into place. He cursed beneath his breath and she watched as he strolled across the rustic-looking kitchen. She liked the tight way his worn blue jeans hugged his ass.

"Very nice," she breathed.

When he disappeared down the hall, she gazed around the room.

The coziness of the pine floor and matching pine dining table and chair reached deep into her soul, soothing her. She loved the open concept of living room, dining room and kitchen. A gorgeous stone fireplace took up one entire corner of the living room and dark brown wood beams crisscrossed the white painted ceiling.

Colorful rugs had been placed on the floor and a couple of chocolate-brown colored leather sofas were set in the middle of the living room with a lovely coffee table situated between them.

She could see herself raising a family here. Safe and friendly and so homey. She grimaced at that idea. Raise a family? Ha! Who in their right mind would want her? She was a convict who'd probably already screwed up her chance here. Suddenly she wanted to cry.

"There, are you satisfied? Now drink your coffee." His brisk voice ripped her back to reality and she gazed up at him. Her sadness vanished.

Oh my, yes, a very tall cowboy. He wore a black cowboy hat. Sexy hot. She shivered involuntarily at his dangerously seductive gaze. Gosh, she wouldn't mind having some raunchy and rough sex-in-a saddle with him.

Wow, normally she wouldn't give having sex with a man a second thought, especially with being locked up in prison. But her thoughts were changing big time now that she was out.

"You are very handsome in a cowboy hat," she blurted. Oh gosh, she was being so bold.

His eyes widened with surprise and his dark eyebrows raised.

Yes, she liked his reaction and she liked being bold.

"Drink the coffee, sweetheart."

Sweetheart. How sweet.

Emotions, thick and raw clutched at her heart. Hot tears bubbled into her eyes, blurring her vision. No guy had spoken so softly and tenderly to her. Ever.

"Shit. Don't cry," he grumbled.

"I'm not. I never cry." At least not in front of people. Dammit, she wasn't about to start now. Angrily, she wiped away her tears with the back of her hands. Thankfully, new tears didn't follow and she struggled to take off her mittens, but they just wouldn't come off.

"Let me help you." His voice was a gentle whisper. His fingers, strong-looking and tanned, grabbed the tips of both mitts and yanked them off her hands.

"Oh, you are so strong," she purred. She wouldn't mind having those long fingers smoothing over her breasts.

"Maybe I should put you to bed. You can sleep it off," he muttered.

"A roll in the hay? It sounds wonderful."

He scowled and she couldn't stop herself from giggling. And hiccupping.

"Okay, that's enough. Let's go." He grabbed her elbow and she let him pull her to her feet.

Yes, he was a big fellow. Was he as big between his thighs? She chuckled at that thought and allowed him to maneuver her down the hallway she'd come in earlier. He stopped at a knotty pine wood door.

Huh. No bars. Cool.

He opened the door, flipped on the lights and ushered her inside.

"Oh my gosh, it's beautiful in here," she whispered. The room followed the log-beamed ceiling theme from the other area of the house. A large stone fireplace, similar to the one in the living room, took up a corner in the room. A cozy fire flickered in the hearth.

The room was sparsely decorated with a large pine bed, a rustic dresser and a large oval rug on the floor. Warmth whipped through her as she spied the blue-and-white gingham curtains that hung on the three windows. Puffy dark-blue pillows and comforters were on the bed. It looked sharp. Wow, he had similar taste to hers.

"This room is really, really, really beautiful," she whispered again and sat down on the bed.

By the wonderment in her voice, Brady knew she truly meant it. For a split second he felt sorry for her. There were a heck of a lot more extravagant rooms than this one in the world, but what else would he expect her to say? She'd just been released from prison. Any room without bars would probably look good to her.

He clamped down on his emotions and hardened his heart.

"Don't get too comfortable, miss."

The severe frown that followed his words made him feel as if he'd just kicked a puppy. He regretted what he'd said immediately. Her perfectly shaped eyebrows had dipped, her forehead furrowed and she looked devastated.

Shit. He hadn't meant to hurt her. Suddenly he just wanted to see her dimples again.

"Listen, we can talk in the morning."

That seemed all the encouragement she needed for she was smiling again and his breath was backing up at the sight of her cute dimples.

"Oh, why don't you sit on the bed with me?" Before he could protest, she'd pulled him down. On top of her!

Wow, she was more powerful than she looked and a hell of a lot more curvy too. Even through the layers of clothing, he could feel her luscious curves. Full breasts pressed against his chest and heat wrapped around his lower half. His cock jerked and hardened and his balls quickly swelled.

She must have felt his reaction, because she suddenly giggled and blinked prettily at him.

"You really aren't as shy as you look, are you?" she asked.

Oh man, she was way too sexy. Almost irresistible. Her lips were lush and red and slightly parted. The wine she'd indulged in smelled pretty good on her breath and the combination of her lips and the wine made him heady with need.

She was staring at him now. Not saying a word. Her big brown eyes were so expressive.

Kiss me, they said to him. *Kiss me.*

He didn't even realize he was lowering his head until her hand slid against the nape of his neck and her warm lips innocently pressed against his.

Heat stroked along his body. Longing burst deep in his belly. He deepened the kiss, wanting more from her. A tremor rocked through her. His shaft shuddered against his jeans. He needed more from her.

Whoa! He needed to put on the brakes. Reluctantly, he broke the kiss.

"Wow, I must be dreaming," she whispered softly and licked her lips.

"You and me both," he said softly.

Oh hell, he was dreaming. No woman had kissed him so tenderly before. So innocently.

The sound of footsteps clomping into the ranch house down the hall broke the magnetic cocoon she'd woven around him.

"Get some sleep," he whispered.

Despite her eyes begging for another kiss, she merely nodded. He sighed and cursed his erection for throbbing so much that he doubted he could even walk.

Get off her!

Yet he couldn't move. Her warm curves hugged his body and he could feel her heart beating frantically against his chest. She was as excited as he was, but she was drunk. He had to get the hell away from her.

"The guys are back. I'd better go."

Again, she nodded. He resisted taking off his cowboy hat and placing it on top of her luscious brown hair. He'd bet she would look sexy as sin wearing it.

He could feel her hot gaze on him as he moved off her and stood. He didn't want to leave. But he had to.

Reluctantly he turned and walked to the door. When he reached it, he hesitated. The sudden urge to tell her that she could stay in his bed for as long as she wanted made him turn around.

To his surprise, she was already asleep. She'd curled herself into the fetal position, her knees drawn up to her belly and her hands tucked beneath her cheeks. Her eyes were closed and a sweet smile played with her lips.

She looked vulnerable. Way too vulnerable. Something raw and wild unleashed from somewhere deep inside of him and for some crazy insane reason he wanted to know everything about her.

He inhaled a deep breath to steady his pounding heart. His lips still tingled from her kiss and he really wanted to kiss her again. Man, she was potent.

He continued to gaze at her. She still wore her coat and her boots. He should get them off her to make her more comfortable, but he didn't want to wake her. She might get chilled during the night, so he grabbed some quilts out of his closet and carefully placed several over her. He held his breath as he touched the zipper on her coat and slowly slid it down until it opened.

He tried to ignore the sweet swell of her breasts peeking out from the V-neck of the green sweater she wore beneath her coat, but the visual was doing some mighty pleasing things to his cock. He wondered if she would wake up if he did give her one more kiss?

From down the hallway, Dan called out his name. Brady cursed softly beneath his breath.

No, he didn't want her to awake again. He needed her gone.

"What the hell is it?" Brady asked softly as he joined Rafe and Dan in the living room.

Rafe noted Brady's flushed face and wondered what the hell he'd been up to, but he'd ask him later. Right now they had other things to attend to. Like the three boxes that had been transported along with the woman.

Rafe pointed to the boxes which Dan and he had opened. They'd assumed their food supplies had been delivered, but the boxes contained everything but food.

"Christmas ornaments. From this note from your sister, she picked them out for us." Dan said as he handed Brady a sealed letter addressed to Brady that they'd found placed inside one of the boxes.

"I'd say it's because of what happened last Christmas," Rafe reminded them. "Remember she stayed for a few days before Christmas and was disappointed that there was no tree?"

"I remember," Brady snarled.

He went silent as he tore open the envelope and then read the note. His frown deepened.

"The little bitch," Brady said softly. "She says she couldn't find two guys to replace Mrs. Wilson at such short notice so we'll have to teach this woman the ropes of what we want her to do around the ranch. Jenna says she's going on vacation for a few weeks and can't be reached. I cannot fucking believe this. Who goes on vacation when she's got her own ranch to run and Cowboys Online too? I don't believe her. We've been fucking set up!"

Brady cursed again and crunched the letter and tossed it over the fireplace screen into the fire. He looked really pissed. Well, he was going to get a hell of a lot nastier.

"There's something else you need to see," Rafe dug into his pocket and withdrew the items they'd found. He handed them to Brady.

"Prescription pills? Any ideas what they are for?" Brady mumbled. His brow furrowed with concern.

Dan, who'd done a short stint in pharmaceutical school after graduating from high school, answered quickly.

"In laymen's terms, one is an anti-anxiety med and the other is a sedative. Mixed with alcohol, it makes one, shall we say, loopy. It can be quite the dangerous mix."

"Loopy?"

"Tipsy, happy, bolder than normal. Like she's acting tonight. I don't think she drank too much or things would have gone downhill by now," Dan said and then he looked toward the staircase. "Will she be joining us for supper?"

Rafe read the excitement in Dan's voice, felt it sift through himself as well. He wouldn't mind getting another look at their new housekeeper and cook. She was very cute and she made his insides warm.

"She's in my room."

She was in Brady's room?

"You move fast, my man," Dan chuckled.

Brady visibly tensed and Rafe prepared himself for an explosion. Lately, Brady was snapping at the both of them. He needed to get laid. They all needed to get laid.

"I didn't want to chance her falling down the stairs. Lawsuit, ever hear of them? She's in my room for the night. I'll take the couch and keep an eye on her tonight. She's asleep."

Dan winked at Rafe. Yeah, they could have a field day with that comment, but his stomach growled and Rafe's did too. Now was not the time to get Brady so pissed that he would toss them out into the snow and lock the doors.

By the way Dan was grinning, Rafe suspected he was about to let loose a volley of inappropriate comments about the woman and Rafe being alone in his bedroom and why was she sleeping instead of peeling off Brady's clothes.

Rafe's cock stiffened at that idea. The three of them had had their share of ménages with willing women.

Rafe clapped his hands and captured both men's attention. "Good! Let's eat!"

JJ moaned softly as something hot and moist clamped over both of her nipples. Sweet suctioning sensations had her gasping and gyrating her hips. She tried to close her thighs but something held them apart.

Heat and pressure melted over her pussy. Slurping sounds whispered through the air. Something, a finger, slid into her vagina. Her muscles eagerly clenched the intruder. She wanted it deeper. Wanted it thrusting into her.

She creamed and cried out as it withdrew and rubbed sensuously over her clitoris. Arousal seared nerve endings. She bucked and panted beneath an onslaught of pleasure.

Heat and desperation snapped through her like a live wire. She needed to be fucked. Wanted to be impaled. She was so primed for penetration that she could scream.

A hot hand smoothed over her belly. A man groaned. The guttural sound was erotic as it spilled into the air. The suctioning on her nipples intensified. She jerked in response to the sensations created.

She slowly blinked her eyes open.

Huh? What was happening? She should be scared, shouldn't she? But she wasn't. Fevered heat whipped through her and she wanted to dive into the agonizing pleasure wrapping around her body.

Flickering lights shone across the walls from a fire in the hearth.

She arched her hips and wrapped her legs around whomever was down there lapping at her pussy. She dug her heels into a hard, muscular back.

Was it that hunky cowboy with the black cowboy hat dining on her? She'd loved his blue eyes and the dark shadow of stubble lining his jaw. Sexy.

Just thinking of him sent ecstasy rocking through her. She gasped at the incredible onslaught of shudders that gripped her. Her fingers knotted into the soft material of the quilt. She clamped her thighs around the intruder.

His lips greedily sucked at her labia. Her belly clenched. She creamed.

His mouth melted over her pussy and his tongue stroked her clit. She bucked as she exploded and was quickly swept into a vortex of pleasure. Her thigh muscles trembled and her nipples ached as the suction increased.

He dipped two fingers into her wet pussy and thrust quickly. She keened and jerked as her muscles clenched tightly around the intrusion. The climax was endless.

She tossed and bucked and shuddered. Her senses were dazed when the orgasm ebbed.

She managed to peer down and gasped as she watched the two male mouths latched to her nipples. Lips eagerly sucked. They wore cowboy hats, but she could see their faces. They were the very nice-looking men she'd seen in the kitchen. Tall guys. She'd liked the way they'd looked at her, first with surprise and then with erotic interest.

They lapped at her with their tongues and pleasure swiftly burst through her again. Shivers lashed her and she convulsed and gyrated her hips, wanting more.

"What's happening?" she whispered. *Why are you doing this to me*? *Why do I love this so much*?

Tongues flicked against her nipples, making them wonderfully sore. Teeth nipped and lips kissed tenderly.

Whoever was going down on her was doing a fantastic job. A rough tongue eagerly lapped at her pussy and lips sucked her engorged clit.

Heat blistered into her. Perspiration beaded on her forehead. Her body tightened again and her breathing quickened. She trembled violently as spasms of pleasure burst through her.

The men didn't stop as she shook and moaned. Their hands slid sensually over her arms, her belly and her breasts. Callused fingers caressed her everywhere until she was a writhing mess of bliss.

Heavens, she was going to climax again!

JJ awoke on a moan. Cold sweat ran down her back and a headache split her skull. She groaned as she flopped onto her back and grimaced at the sound of her heart pounding in her ears. When she opened her eyes, an unfamiliar room came into focus and a wagon wheel chandelier hung from the ceiling right above her.

She blinked in surprise. Where was she? She wasn't in a prison cell anymore?

Then it all rushed back to her. How she'd struggled against panicking in the small confines of that unbelievably small plane. Realizing the prescription drugs she'd taken were barely keeping her calm. Seeing that case of red wine. Grabbing a bottle and twisting the cap...kissing a very sexy cowboy with blue eyes wearing a black cowboy hat.

Her tummy hollowed out with a very nice feeling. That kiss must have been part of a dream. And what a dream it had been. Three cowboys making love to her.

She resisted the urge to reach down and slip her fingers between her thighs and touch herself like the delicious cowboys had been touching her. Any other time and she would have masturbated and enjoyed the feelings that the awesome dream had created.

But she was not in the privacy of her cell and even if she had been, her cellmate could have heard. She'd always had to wait until the woman snored up a storm before she'd masturbate. Thankfully those days were over...she vaguely remembered coming into this room though...

She sat up and gazed around. Dim light filtered into the room through the windows. She remembered the blue-and-white curtains.

She glanced at the bedside table. A travel alarm clock ticked loudly. It was three minutes after seven.

She winced as the headache continued to pound against her temples. Her tummy felt a bit queasy. Pain meds would come in handy for her headache. She could use a nice cold shower too. Gosh, she was still fully clothed and sweating.

She froze when her gaze fell upon the black cowboy hat settled on a nearby dresser.

No freaking way.

Had she *really* kissed that cowboy? More memories began to trickle back. A gorgeous blue-eyed man with a severe frown. He'd studied her so intently while she sat on her suitcases on that landing strip, or had it been a lake?

Her gut clenched. She'd been drunk.

Embarrassment washed over her. She needed to apologize for her behavior and explain. But she'd kissed a cowboy. Maybe he'd just been a hired hand? Oh, she seriously hoped so.

Excitement whipped through her as she remembered the rock-hard erection pressing against her pussy right after she'd dragged him on top of her on the bed. His blue eyes had darkened as he'd looked at her. A nervous muscle in his jaw had twitched. His warm breath had caressed her lips so sweetly she'd practically been begging him for a kiss.

And what a kiss they'd shared. Electricity had snapped through her as his mouth touched hers. Her body had come alive beneath his hardness and an insistent need to be fucked by him had swept over her. She blew out a tense breath and jumped as wind battered against the windows. Frost edged the glass and snow swirled outside. A snowstorm?

She moaned as she climbed out from beneath layers of snuggly quilts. She cursed her splitting headache as she stood.

Had that cowboy she'd kissed covered her with these quilts?

Oh darn. She'd given those men such a bad impression upon her arrival. Why had she drank so much wine? She should have known she'd be hungover. And mixing alcohol with drugs. So very dangerous.

She shook her head. She'd been so stupid. She would never let something like that happen again.

She gazed out one of the bedroom windows. Surprise washed over her. Everything was whiter than when she'd arrived last night. The trees. The barn, sheds and fences were all drenched in snow. Through the swirling flakes, she spied the lake. It was huge. It stretched for miles.

Talk about a desolate place, but very pretty too.

She moved away from the window and tiptoed in her boots to the closed door and listened. Silence. Maybe everybody was still sleeping?

She opened the door and walked into a short hallway. Thankfully, the bathroom was right across the hall from the bedroom and she quickly scooted inside. Horror raced through her as she gazed into a mirror. Dark circles were smudged beneath her eyes and her shoulder-length dark-brown hair was a tangled mess.

She quickly grabbed a comb off a nearby shelf and had the mass tamed within a couple of minutes. She wished she had makeup, but Sabrina had said there would be none in the suitcases. There would be clothing, some cash and nothing else. Before leaving the prison with Sabrina, she'd been given this parka, warm boots, hat and mittens, along with the two suitcases with the clothes that she hadn't had a chance to investigate.

Speaking of the suitcases, she needed to find them, grab that shower and change into a fresh set of clothing.

After washing her face and going to the bathroom, she felt reasonably refreshed and a bit more confident to face the world. In the medicine cabinet she found painkillers, and took two pills.

A bubble of emotions flared inside her at the sudden thought that she was now out of prison and on her own. She pushed the unwanted fear aside, braced her shoulders and opened the bathroom door.

Why was it so quiet? At the prison it had always been loud. Even at night when women would cry out in their nightmares or moan while they masturbated in their cells, it was noisy.

Now it seemed as if she'd gone from one extreme to the other. It was a bit unnerving.

She stepped into the hallway and wandered to the end of the hall where she discovered the cute open concept living room, dining room and kitchen that she'd been in last night. She remembered thinking how rustic and homey it looked.

Cowboy-country comfortable. A feeling of warmth and of being embraced moved through her. She'd experienced the same sensation yesterday upon arriving here. Was she crazy thinking that this might be her forever place?

The aromatic scent of coffee encouraged her to seek out the coffee machine. It was located on the kitchen counter. To her surprise there was also a note propped against the coffeemaker. The note was addressed to her.

JJ

Your suitcases are in the upstairs bedroom. First door on your right.

Make yourself at home. We'll be back around lunch.

Dan

Was he the guy who she'd so boldly pulled onto her after she'd plopped onto the bed?

Oh boy. She had been a bad girl last night, but relief poured through her. She would have a bit of time to catch her breath and absorb everything, and she'd start with that coffee.

Chapter Three

"Well, that's the last of the hay," Dan said as he climbed down the ladder from the hayloft and placed the pitchfork on a nearby hook. He shoved his gloves into his jacket pockets and strolled to where Brady were brushing hay off his clothes.

Brady had always been a bit of a gruff guy—except after he got himself laid. But since the arrival of the cute chick last night, he'd been biting their heads off at every turn.

"It better be the last time that stack falls over, because it's pissing me off," Brady growled at him. White puffs of air floated out of his mouth as he spoke and his face was once again red.

Just like last night. Great.

"The horses are fed and watered and the manure is taken care of. All the stalls are clean," Rafe said as he rounded the corner from the stall area where they kept their horses and joined them.

Dan caught Rafe's gaze and tossed him a teasing wink.

"I guess there's no more excuses to stay out of the ranch house, is there?" Dan was barely able to keep himself from laughing.

On cue, Brady bristled.

Yes, that woman had definitely gotten under Brady's skin. Maybe he was attracted to her?

"Wonder if she's awake yet. It will be nice to finally meet her. Kind of like you did last night, Brady," Rafe added with a wink.

Dan grinned as Brady frowned and gazed around the interior of the barn. If Dan didn't miss his guess, he'd think Brady was looking for more work for them to do. Perhaps it was time to get serious with the guy?

"Stall much?" Dan prodded.

"I am not stalling," he shot back. "There's still plenty of work to be done. You guys go ahead. I'll be in shortly."

The lights flickered as a blast of wind buffeted the walls of the barn.

"Oh, oh," Dan said as he gazed up at the lights hanging from the barn ceiling. They flickered again. Then the barn dropped into darkness.

Damn.

A couple of pregnant cows close to giving birth mooed their distress from nearby stalls and then they fell silent.

"I'll get the barn generators going. You two head over to the house and get the house generator going so she doesn't get scared," Brady ordered.

Oh, so he *did* care about the woman. That was a very good sign.

It took them only a couple of minutes to follow the rope they'd put up between the house and the barn. The rope was a lifeline during snowstorms and power outages. Winters were brutal up north. During storms one could barely see their hand in front of their face and getting lost was not an option. One froze to death rather quickly without a fire.

The snow was already more than ankle deep as he and Rafe headed for the house. Cold snowflakes stung his face as he stomped up the stairs. When he opened the back door and stepped into the mudroom, a smoky aroma of overdone bacon drifted beneath his nostrils. His stomach growled.

Hmm, bacon for lunch. He liked this girl already.

"Smells good," Rafe commented as they both kicked off their boots and then their winter coats and hung them on the hooks lining one wall of the mudroom.

Suddenly he heard the woman curse and Rafe nudged Dan and smiled.

"She's our kind of lady," Rafe quipped. He dragged his blue wool hat off his head, then quickly combed his fingers through his medium-length, dark-brown hair, looking a bit self-conscious.

"She sounds feisty," Dan said with a laugh.

They opened the glass storm door that separated the main ranch and the mudroom. A moment later they entered the kitchen. It was eerily gray inside without lights.

JJ stood by the stove, a frying pan in her hand. A thin wisp of blue smoke trailed from it. She continued to curse as she stared longingly at the light fixture in the kitchen.

Yeah, she was a pretty one. Her hair was dark brown, shoulder-length and a mass of curls. She wore snug blue jeans and a tight blouse that silhouetted perky breasts. She was thin and he supposed that had to do with lousy prison food.

"It's a good thing the electricity went out when it did. The smoke alarms would have kicked in soon." Dan said as he eyed the wispy smoke drifting out of the pan.

At the sound of his voice, her brown eyes widened in surprise and she screeched as if she'd seen a couple of mice.

"A good thing she's not jumpy, or lunch would be all over the floor," Rafe commented with a grin.

Her brow furrowed and she frowned, suddenly looking shy.

"Sorry we scared you. I'm Dan, this is Rafe. We're partners in the ranch."

Dan stretched out his hand.

She smiled. His breath caught as dimples popped out in her cheeks making her even prettier. She deposited the pan on the stove, rubbed her hands on a towel, and then slipped her palm against his and squeezed his fingers.

Her smile widened and her handshake was firm and confident. He liked that.

"Hi, I'm JJ and I apologize for last night," she said quickly.

Dan liked the way her cheeks suddenly flushed a pretty pink.

"Sorry for what? Exactly what happened between you and Brady last night?" he teased.

She pulled her hand from his grip, acting as if it was suddenly on fire. Huh, interesting reaction. So, something did happen between the two of them and that's why Brady was acting so weird and not wanting to come into the house.

"Ignore Dan's rudeness. Pleased to meet you, JJ," Rafe said and quickly shook hands with her.

Yep, that was Rafe, always the diplomatic one.

She really was pretty. Not one ounce of makeup on her and she looked fresh and smelled a whole lot better than any other woman he'd ever met. And there had been several women here over the years who enjoyed ménages with the three of them as well as one on ones. He wondered if JJ was that kind of liberated?

He doubted it, from that blush still lingering on her cheeks. He found it difficult to comprehend she'd been in prison for murder, but that's what the application had said.

She looked quite young. She would be inexperienced sexually, so there was no use in even thinking about her in that way. Despite those thoughts, he couldn't help but fantasize about teaching her how good sexual pleasure could be at the hands of three experienced men instead of just an awkward teenage one. That was, if she'd any experiences before she'd gone to prison.

Besides, he might never find out much about her, because if Brady had his way, she was leaving on the next flight out. If they could get an answer from Jenna, who'd conveniently not answered her cell last night—which made him wonder if maybe she had been telling the truth in her letter and she really *had* gone off on vacation. As far as he could remember the only other vacation she'd taken in years was last Christmas when she'd come to visit them here.

"I'm a little inexperienced in the cooking department," she admitted shyly. Her eyes glistened with enjoyment and apology.

Innocent amusement. It appeared she had no idea how a man could perceive a comment like the one she'd just given.

Beside him Rafe cleared his throat, and Dan had the impression Rafe was thinking exactly the same thing. She'd been out of the sexual loop for quite some time and that idea was making him react.

"I hope you don't mind. I found my suitcases in the upstairs bedroom and I took a shower."

Oh man, visions of her standing naked in the shower, water droplets cascading over perky breasts and... His cock hardened inappropriately and he managed to stifle a growl of excitement before it hit his throat.

"How does one cook without electricity around here? Do I use the fireplace?" she asked. She gazed with wide eyes at the nearest fireplace, which still had some glowing embers.

"Propane generators, and I'll get one of them started. It's just outside the back in a shed," Rafe muttered and made a quick exit, leaving Dan alone with the woman.

Bastard. What was Rafe thinking leaving Dan to fend for himself around a gorgeous, do-not-touch, sexually inexperienced woman?

"We use the fireplaces to cook as a last resort. Since a fire adds a bit of cheeriness during snowstorms, we keep one going in here during the day and each of the bedroom fireplaces during the night." Dan replied as he gazed at her. Yup, she was very pretty and he needed to keep his mind off the sexual things he'd like to do with her. Time to get that fire going and he didn't mean the one that was already igniting within him.

"That's rustic, and this house is gorgeous too," she said with a smile as he brushed past her and headed for the fireplace.

"All three of us had input in the designs of the entire ranch, so we're pretty proud," he said as an inner glow flowed through him at her compliment.

He tossed some birch bark, a few pieces of dry kindling and a split pine log on the fire. Orange flames immediately crackled along the birch and lapped at the wood. The fire breathed back to life, heating his hands.

"Oh! That's how it's done," she said from immediately behind him.

Shit! He hadn't heard her approach.

He straightened and faced her. Curiosity and excitement flared in her eyes. She had very dark brown eyes with pretty little flecks of gold in them. The defiant tilt to her chin gave him the impression she was eager to learn about their ranch, and her sexy, flowery scent whispered beneath his nostrils, awakening nerve endings. His cock throbbed achingly. He hadn't felt like this since he was a teenager.

He frowned. This was not the reaction to her that he had expected. Not at all.

Oh man, now he understood why Brady was acting like an irritated black bear. The three of them never mixed business with pleasure, knowing the consequences would not be good. Having JJ around was sorely going to push their limits and their self-imposed law.

Brady was right. Maybe it was best if she was on the next available flight out of here.

Rafe and Dan were so extremely helpful and polite that JJ immediately fell in love with them. It was as if she'd known them her entire life. They were easy to be around and nice eye-candy. She also found it difficult not to blush and to not think about the ménage dream she'd experienced, with them as her star lovers.

Rafe was the taller of the two men. His hair was a medium-length dark brown with wisps curling along his neckline. He had dark-brown eyes, a nose slightly off-center—which most likely meant it had been broken at one point and not set properly.

What drew most of her attention to Rafe was his quiet, peaceful nature. He calmed her with his soft voice and casual attitude.

Dan was cute too. And funny. He made her laugh a lot. He wore his hair a bit longer than Rafe, but Dan's hair was wavy and a light brown and he had dark-green eyes that reminded her of forest green. Both men had scruffy five o'clock shadows that lined their cheeks and jaws.

They wore plaid flannel t-shirts and tight blue jeans that cupped very sensuously curved asses. Butts that reminded her of the missing cowboy. The one who'd kissed her so sweetly last night that she continued to blush even into the early afternoon every time she thought about the kiss and him.

But where was he? She didn't want to appear interested, so she made it a point not to ask Rafe or Dan as they showed her around the ranch house room by room. As it turned out she'd slept last night in her boss' bedroom.

Gosh, he probably thought she was some kind of drunk and hated her for stealing his bed. She had so much to apologize to him for that she almost wished she'd never have to see him again.

Rafe and Dan showed her were the food was located in the pantry, as well as the small root cellar in the basement and the two large freezers in the mudroom. They also gave her a quick tour of the generator shed just outside the ranch house, where one of two huge generators purred quietly.

The laundry room came next. It was located just off the mudroom, beside their office and down the hall from the bedroom she'd slept in last night. The laundry room had plenty of windows, two washers and two dryers. She noted an outdoor clothesline that stretched from an outside platform and disappeared into the swirling snow.

Odd, too, that being trapped here in a snowstorm didn't set off a panic attack or the feeling of claustrophobia. She hadn't felt this free since—well, she didn't know since when.

For lunch, she tossed out the burned bacon and the guys taught her how not to burn it. Then they ate bacon and cheese sandwiches, and as per their request, she brewed lots of coffee. By the time they left to do their respective chores, she felt confident she knew where all the food supplies were stored.

For supper, she'd been instructed to warm up leftover bear stew in the fridge and to surprise them with dessert.

The house was quiet without them around and she discovered she really loved the peace. Yes, she wouldn't mind settling down here and working for these guys. Wouldn't mind it at all.

"What the hell is going on in here?" Brady muttered as he entered the living room and gazed at the miniature Christmas lights blinking at a couple of the frost-encrusted windows and then surveyed green garland woven with twinkling lights cascading over the fireplace mantel.

He'd remained in the barn most of the afternoon, finding all kinds of things to keep himself busy. He'd helped a cow deliver her first calf and kept an eye on them both until he was sure the cow and calf would get along. Most of all, he tried to keep his mind off the woman in his ranch house. But his growling stomach had finally forced him to find food.

At his gruff voice, the woman looked up from where she sat on the sofa inspecting the open boxes his sister had sent. When the woman saw him, her mouth formed a sweet o, and guilt chased across her pretty features. She immediately stood.

"I'm sorry. Was I not supposed to break into the Christmas stuff yet? Dan and Rafe said it was okay, but if it's not..."

"It's fine." Why the hell did his voice sound so grumpy and loud?

No wonder she looked startled and uneasy. Damn, this was so not how he wanted her reacting around him.

"I get in a bad mood when I'm hungry." The words were out of his mouth before he could stop them. He hoped she didn't think he meant sexually hungry, because he did.

Oh great! She was on his mind again.

"Supper is just about ready. I have it warming on the stove, and the coffee is just brewing. The fellows are upstairs showering."

Damn, he really liked the musical sound of her voice.

She bit her lower lip as a shy look flashed into her brown eyes. She was cute. Too damn cute for a rough guy like him.

"Listen, um. I'd like to apologize for last night," she said softly. "I got into the wine because I was hoping it would help soothe my nerves. I just don't like flying."

So that was it. Yeah, she could be lying to cover up, but he could plainly see she was sincere.

"Don't worry about it." Why had he just said that? He'd been rehearsing all day about telling her it wasn't going to work out and that she would have to leave as soon as he could arrange it. Yet one look at her sweetly shaped body and her eyes full of excitement as she gazed longingly at the Christmas ornaments tucked away in the boxes, and he was folding as if he had a bad hand in a game of cards.

Shit. If she left here, she'd probably have to go back to prison. That idea shocked him. Her, in the prison system? For ten years? She looked too young to be a convict.

"How about some coffee?" She said with a smile. His courage to oust her caved as her pretty dimples popped into her cheeks.

He nodded and strolled toward the coffee machine, pleased that she'd already been trained in the art of having coffee available before they started eating supper. Maybe his devious sister did know what she was doing by sending JJ here. Despite that, he would be giving her a ton of shit when she decided to pick up her phone.

"Please, you sit at the table and I'll serve you coffee," she said softly.

She'd come up behind him and her fresh scent had him inhaling slowly and savoring her smell. Reluctantly, he moved away from her and took his spot at the head of the table.

"It's a beautiful knotty pine table," she said a moment later as she set a steaming mug of black coffee in front of him. Then she stroked the top of the table with her fingers. He liked the tender way she did that.

Pride flowed through him. He liked the smooth-planked dining table. It was a good fifteen feet long and three feet wide. It had been polished until the knots shone and then he and his two friends had stained the wood until it gave a golden hue.

"The guys and I designed it. We made it from a couple of the pine trees off our land. We have a sawmill in behind one of the barns and we enjoy making furniture. We made pretty much every stick of wooden furniture in this house."

"I love everything. It's rustic and very easy on the eyes."

"It's not too masculine for you?" Why had he asked her that question?

"No, not all. I've never seen such beauty in my life. Everything here is just perfect."

Huh, she was the first woman who'd ever said that.

He kept watching her fingers as she kept touching the table. She had pretty fingernails. Cut short and no fancy nail polish. He liked that she wasn't into all that makeup and beautifying stuff.

"Rafe and Dan said that you guys hired people to build the ranch house and that they culled the wood for the walls from the forest?"

When she noticed he'd been watching her hand, she stopped stroking the table and knotted her hands in front of her. She was still a bit nervous. He didn't blame her. It was her first day on the job.

"Yep, they were flown in with their chainsaws and axes and they built the house from the trees from the nearby forest. They put the house together the way we'd designed it. Then the electrician and plumber came in and they did their magic. The hydro people and phone people strung their lines and we were in business. Right now, with the electricity out, we have generators as a backup, but we're planning on getting solar panels for the roofs in a year or two."

"Impressive."

An uneasy silence enveloped the air and he took a sip of his coffee. The steaming liquid tasted bitter and strong, just the way he liked it.

"Um, I really want to assure you that what happened last night won't happen again," she said quietly.

Damn, was she talking about her being drunk? Or that wicked kiss they'd shared? To his shock, his cheeks warmed as he remembered the sweet way her mouth had opened beneath his aggression. Man, he hadn't blushed since he'd been a teenager.

"I'm sure things will be fine," he replied and quickly took another sip of the scalding liquid.

Thankfully, she moved away and headed back to the living room.

"So how do you like your Christmas decorations? Rafe and Dan said your sister Jenna sent them. I think she has exquisite taste."

Apparently she wasn't looking for an answer, because she'd already returned to the sofa and began to investigate her boxes.

Her boxes.

She acted like a kid at Christmas. Her eyes were wide with wonder as she lifted a delicate glass angel from one of the boxes.

"This is one of my favorites," she said. She held it up for him to see and the little angel twirled on a gold string. He had to admit the ornament did look quite nice.

"We need a tree," she blurted and gazed at him with complete expectation.

He dared not say no.

"The minute the storm breaks and we catch up on all the chores and checking on the animals that need doing, we'll all go out and cut down a tree."

She smiled at him and her dimples popped gain. His gut somersaulted.

"Did I hear someone mention a Christmas tree?" Dan chuckled as he almost flew down the stairs. Stairs, which Brady noted, also had some of those twinkling white lights dangling from the railing.

He had to admit the lights did look festive, even though they were probably a bit of a drain on their power.

"Brady said we can go look for a tree when the storm is over. Oh!" She suddenly placed a hand over her mouth as a shocked expression whipped across her face.

"I'm sorry. Should I call you Mr...? I don't even know your last name."

"Brady is fine." Dan but in. "We're very informal here."

JJ nodded and wrapped the glass angel into red tissue paper and delicately settled it back into one of the boxes.

Rafe hurried down the stairs. "Smells good! When do we eat? I'm starving," he shouted, rubbing his hands together with supreme expectation.

"You're always hungry," Dan chided as he and Rafe took their seats at the table.

Brady grinned to himself. Rafe's damp hair was slicked back off his forehead and he was wearing one of his better polo shirts.

As a matter of fact, now that he noticed it, Dan looked spiffy and cleaner than usual in a white buttondown shirt. It kind of made Brady feel As if he weren't dressed properly for dinner in his old work shirt and tattered jeans. He'd have to make sure that he looked presentable too, now that they had a beautiful woman in the house.

Yeah, she was really pretty with that mane of dark-brown hair and sweet breasts that pushed against a blouse that seemed almost too tight for her. Suddenly, he got the feeling that she'd been here forever. He shook his head. Now he knew for sure he was being stupid.

They all fell silent and gazed at JJ, who smiled back at them as she hurried to the stove.

"Gentlemen, dinner is served."

Dinner conversation was robust. To her surprise JJ enjoyed serving the men. She loved how easygoing they were and how wonderfully they interacted with each other and spoke about their cattle and the plans for the ranch.

They were like a well-oiled machine. Each man had his own duties and each recounted what they'd done during the day. They spoke about problems they'd encountered and how to solve them or what needed to be done to resolve them.

They were very polite when they addressed her and they were sure to include her by asking her opinions. She truly felt as if she belonged here. It was better than any dream she could ever have come up with.

Despite a rough introduction, everything was turning out to be perfect and she hadn't even been here twenty-four hours!

Dan liked the way JJ fit in here. She'd caught on fast when they'd shown her where everything was located. She'd made great sandwiches at lunch, and she'd insisted they each eat an apple afterward. She hadn't so much as complained as to how desolate it was here, like the other women who'd been here.

She actually appeared to be enjoying it here. Her cheeriness couldn't be faked. He would have thought with her being in prison, she might have needed some adjustment time, especially if she was on those meds they'd found.

But as she served dinner—albeit leftovers—she placed the dishes onto the table with ease and confidence. She was a natural. She belonged here. If Brady brought up the subject of getting rid of her, he would protest and loudly.

From the smile Brady was toting and the grin flirting at the edges Rafe's lips, he doubted he would hear any objections from either of the men. Somewhere between her sitting down at the table to eat with them and her getting up to bring them dessert—which turned out to be whipped chocolate pudding in huge mugs—he realized he wanted this gorgeous woman in his life.

And he didn't mean in an employer-employee relationship. He wanted more. A whole hell of a lot more.

Chapter Four

She reminded Rafe of a little stray kitten.

Last night, when she'd shown up, she'd been lost and out of her element. Today, she appeared confident, happy, and had blossomed into one hell of a sexy woman.

At dinner, he couldn't keep his eyes off her. He had to force himself to concentrate on what Brady and Dan were talking about. When it had been his turn to make a report of his day's work, he'd barely managed to keep himself from bragging at how much work he'd done in transporting hay to the south meadow via the snowmobile and sled to the young free-range Angus cattle that roamed there. The beef were already well-formed and well-insulated with fat. After a good spring and summer, they would bring top dollar as organic beef in the fall.

He enjoyed JJ's curiosity. She asked questions about how they got the cattle to market and he explained they did good old-fashioned cattle drives through forests. There were plenty of rivers for water and lots of green areas, which had been forests. Due to clear-cutting by lumber barons who hadn't replanted, lush meadows thrived in the north country.

Those meadows, rivers and lakes were used for food and drink for the cattle and replenished any weight they would lose during the drive. The cattle were driven to a railway about a hundred miles south of the ranch house. He was glad she didn't grimace or say she felt sorry for the cattle when he mentioned they went via rail to a slaughterhouse and then they were prepared for their special brand of organic beef.

The ranch was their way of life and that's just the way it was with beef cattle. There were plenty of people who swore that their free-range Northern Ontario beef tasted the juiciest on a barbecue grill and they had the robust sales to prove it.

Yeah, she was a really good fit for them and he couldn't wait for Jenna to start picking up her phone so he could thank her for a one hell of a good Christmas gift.

Brady tried like hell to keep his mind focused on what the two other men were saying regarding business. But his mind just kept wandering to JJ and what her succulent scent was doing to his cock. Several times, he'd shifted his ass on the chair to loosen his jeans, which were suddenly way too tight.

He noted the guys were paying attention to her every move, just as he'd been doing. Thankfully, though, they didn't make idiots out of themselves by going all doe-eyed on her and the meal went relatively smoothly. Desert was damn delicious. Chocolate pudding had never tasted so good and he had some mighty fine visions of licking pudding off her nipples and then dabbing some onto her clit and licking it off as he went down on her.

Maybe one day...

After supper, JJ ushered the guys out of the kitchen so she could clean up. They retreated to the adjoining living room, where they quickly began playing cards. Their laughter and loud whoops when one lost or won made her smile. When she'd finished with the dishes and cleaned up, she'd excused herself and retreated to her room, not wanting to intrude on their fun.

She didn't know how long she'd been sitting cross-legged here on the queen-sized bed relishing the rustic red and brown decor, but she still couldn't believe she'd been given such a beautiful room. She kept resisting the urge to pinch herself for fear she would actually wake up and discover that coming here had all been a dream.

Not more than forty-eight hours ago she'd been in a prison cell, locked behind bars, expecting to be there for at least another ten years. Early that the morning, just after breakfast, she'd been summoned to the warden's office. The warden had asked JJ if she still wanted to be a part of the Freedom Run Project. JJ had said yes.

She'd been shocked to discover there was an opening available. She'd almost forgotten she'd applied for a spot more than a year ago, when rumor had drifted through the ranks that such a project had just been newly formed.

She'd immediately gone to the warden, who had given her an application form to fill out. She'd been warned that it could take years. Maybe even never. But she'd put in her name anyway.

There had been an emergency parole hearing that same day, totally unheard of by her prison mates. She'd been stunned when they said yes. She'd been denied parole already twice.

And here she was in this beautiful bedroom with fresh rusty-colored sheets and comforters, a large bed with a gorgeous pine headboard and matching pine furniture.

She loved the setup of this house. Her room had its own bathroom and shower. They'd given her the bedroom closest to the stairs which would allow her to sneak out down in the morning to get the day started. She already had all the chores planned out in her head as she sat in the middle of her queen-sized bed, staring at the rustic decor and immersing herself in the flattering shades of reds and browns.

Her suitcases sat at the foot of her bed, open but unpacked from when she'd quickly gone through them this morning to find something suitable to wear after showering.

Whoever had purchased the clothing and necessities had bought everything one size too small. So her clothing was a bit snug. But she didn't care. She was free.

A knock at the door had her telling whomever was there to come on in. She hadn't even thought to get up off the bed. Hadn't even thought to go to the door and open it herself.

The door opened and Brady stood there. He didn't come in. He looked a bit hesitant, maybe even shy.

"You forgot your purse. I thought you might need it." He dropped it on the chair that sat right beside the open doorway.

"Thanks, I appreciate it." She had forgotten that she'd brought it downstairs after she'd showered because she'd thought she'd needed to keep her meds close. Just in case. Surprisingly, she hadn't even remembered them.

"Thanks."

She thought he would leave but when he continued to stand there and stare at her, she realized he had something else he wanted to say. Perhaps he'd seen the meds? The purse was open.

"I have claustrophobia. I don't handle plane rides well or anything that confines me. That's why I have prescription pills," she confessed.

Although she had explained her problem to him earlier today, he still appeared surprised.

"Did you get that problem because you were in prison? Being in a cell would probably do a number on most people."

She hesitated, not wanting to go into it. But then she quickly decided he should know the truth. Or at least a bit of it.

"Actually, no. I had that problem before I went in." She wished she could say more, but it had been such a lovely day, she didn't want to end it by bringing up awful memories of what had happened with her stepfather. He'd been a cop with a discipline complex. Anytime she did something wrong, he'd beat her and lock her in a dark basement closet as punishment. That was when she'd begun to have her anxiety and claustrophobia issues. At first her mother had vehemently protested the abuse, but too many beatings from her new husband had quietened her.

When Brady didn't ask any further questions, she quickly changed the subject.

"How long have you three lived here?"

"Seven years," he answered with a smile. She'd noticed earlier that he enjoyed talking about his ranch and the furniture they'd made.

"And you guys don't get lonely?" Oh dear, where had that question come from?

"I mean, I'm assuming there aren't any close neighbors. No places to go out and dance or socialize or…"

He suddenly looked a bit irritated. Maybe even disappointed?

"You're making the place sound like a prison cell. If you don't think you'll be happy here…"

Panic rocked her. Did he want her gone?

"Oh my gosh. No, please don't get the wrong idea. I love this place. I love the snowstorm and the wilderness. Everything is so beautiful." She waved her hands at the room. "I couldn't have asked for a more beautiful room."

To her surprise, he grinned.

Sweet shivers scrambled up her spine. She loved the sensual curve of his lips. Loved that he seemed pleased that she liked it here.

"Listen, if you can't take the solitude, please let me know. My sister can find you another placement and then you wouldn't have to go back to prison. So please don't say you like it here because you may be afraid you have to go back there."

Oh wow, he could read her like a book.

"Seriously, I do love it here. I would like it if you guys would give me a try."

He nodded.

"Okay then. In case the guys didn't tell you, we shut the generators off to consume electricity at nine. If you want to keep the lights on, there are oil lamps and matches." He nodded to a pine shelf with two oil lamps.

"Just keep them away from the blankets and don't fall asleep with them on. And if you need a flashlight, there's one in the nightstand beside your bed."

"Thanks for the warning on the lights."

"Oh, and about the fireplace..." He strolled into her room and headed to the fireplace. Gosh, he had big shoulders. He made her bedroom suddenly seem as if it was much smaller, but in a nice cozy kind of way.

"I'll get the fire going, so you'll be nice and toasty for a few hours. But it'll be chilly come morning. I turn the generators on at five. We usually have breakfast around five thirty and we're out the door by six. Lunch is usually around eleven and supper at four. I gets dark early during the winter months."

"Good to know. Breakfast will be ready at five thirty." Goodness, they were early risers.

She fell silent as she observed how he scrunched up a piece of paper, set some small pieces of kindling on top, then lit the fire. Orange flames quickly consumed the wood. Then he placed several bigger pieces of firewood on top. He used the same technique as Dan had today while starting the living room fire in the fireplace.

"When the fire gets further along, toss on a couple of split logs. Think you can handle it?"

"I'm no Girl Scout, but I think I can handle it."

"If you need help, just knock on your wall. Rafe's room is on the other side. Or call Dan. He's across the hall. Or come and get me."

"Sure, thanks." She doubted she would bother any of them. She wanted to become as independent as possible to prove to them and herself she was a good employee.

He strolled toward the door.

"Brady?"

He turned. "Yes?"

"When do you think we can get that Christmas tree?"

He smiled again. Gosh, she just loved his smile.

"We'll fit it in. Most likely by this weekend. We'll take out the snowmobiles and hunt for one."

Snowmobiles? Awesome! She'd never been on one before.

"Okay, see you at breakfast." His tone had turned brisk and businesslike again.

"Got it. I forgot to ask. Do you want me to pack you a lunch or will you be coming in for lunch?"

He hesitated, appearing shy again.

"I'll be in for lunch. Good night," he said a moment later.

"Good night."

He nodded and then closed the door softly behind him.

She let out a huge sigh of relief.

Oh my gosh! She wasn't sure why he made her so nervous and so aware of him. She just hoped she didn't have any more hot ménage dreams like she'd had just before waking this morning. If she did, she would find it incredibly difficult to keep her mind on the job. She really wanted this job, because these three guys were as close to family life she'd experienced in a long time.

Brady exhaled a slow breath as he quietly walked away from JJ's bedroom. Finding her sitting cross-legged on her bed, looking totally at ease, as if she belonged here, had shot a powerful jolt of want through him.

Man, he'd never reacted this scorching way to a woman. So out of control with thoughts of wanting to have sex with her. Only her. No other woman.

Damn. How the hell was he going to handle this need?

They knew several ladies who enjoyed ménages. He could call one of them. But those women didn't hold a candle to the way he felt around JJ.

He should go and talk to Dan and Rafe and put out feelers for their reactions to her, but he decided against it. His confession would only bring another round of teasing from Dan and too many questions from Rafe.

He'd deal with this problem on his own. At least for now.

Rafe lay in bed and listened to Brady's footsteps walk away from JJ's bedroom. He'd heard them speaking and wondered what had dared Brady to go to her bedroom.

Man, he'd been trying to find a reason to see her and he'd come up with plenty of them, but he'd chickened out. It was her second night here, and he wondered how in the world he would be able to sleep with her lying in a bed right on the other side of his bedroom wall.

Normally, he didn't go to sleep this early. Neither did Dan. But due to the storm and the electricity being down, he knew lights were out at nine. Since it was Brady's turn to take generator duties this time around, Rafe had opted to tuck himself in early and do a bit of sexual release work. He figured Dan and Brady would be doing their own thing tonight too.

They'd have to be inhuman if they didn't respond to a sexy chick like JJ.

He turned off his bedside lamp, slipped his hands beneath his blankets and wrapped his fingers around his swollen, aching shaft.

Arousal coursed through JJ and she opened her eyes fully aware that someone was in the bedroom with her. Firelight rippled romantically on the walls and ceiling and she gasped softly when she spied Brady, Rafe and Dan. They stood beside each other, in a row, at the foot of her bed, gazing down at her. They wore cowboy hats and nothing else. Muscles rippled over their naked bodies. Each man held his engorged cock in his hand, and each stroked his swollen length with long fingers.

Awareness zinged through her. She hadn't realized the comforters had been pulled off her. Her legs were spread wide, her hand was between her thighs, and she leisurely stroked the small, ultra-sensitive bud of her clit.

Oh my gosh, was she having a dream? Or were they really here?

"Is everything all right?" she whispered.

"We want to make love to you," Brady whispered.

Excitement jolted through her. She creamed and her fingers moved quicker over her clit.

"We can't stop thinking about you," Rafe growled.

She reached up and smoothed her hand over her breasts. Her fingers found a nipple and she pinched it until it hardened and grew sweetly painful and then she moved to her other nipple, doing the same.

"Don't tease us like this, JJ." Dan's voice was raspy and rough.

"You guys are the one teasing me," she breathed.

She blew out a tense breath as they continued staring at her and stroking their engorged cocks. JJ's breathing grew quicker as she rubbed her breasts and massaged her moist clit. Frustrated pleasure swept through her.

The men were off limits. *Look, but don't touch. Fantasize, but don't fuck.*

Wicked heat flared through her as each of their cocks swelled and lengthened in front of her. They looked so hot wearing nothing but their cowboy hats. She wanted to touch their muscles and feel their hardness flex beneath her fingers.

She craved to wrap her hands around each of their shafts and take a cock into her mouth, another one into her pussy and yet another one into her ass. The intense ache deep inside her increased. She yearned to be possessed by them.

She arched her hips and moaned at the visions of being triple-penetrated. Swollen, thick shafts sinking deep inside of her. Hot flesh slapping against her trembling body. Guttural moans of arousal splashing through her bedroom.

"Fuck me," she begged them.

They didn't move. Didn't say a word. They just stood there watching her. Their eyes were dark with lust and need. Their hands were torturously slow as they kneaded their shafts

Her face heated as their gazes drifted to her breasts and then lower. They watched her hand between her thighs as she fingerfucked herself. Her swollen pussy throbbed as she stroked her fingers past the folds and plunged in and out of her vagina with a despaired frenzy.

Oh, damn them! She would do the job herself!

Her breaths grew harsh and fast as her two fingers swept over her clit. She rubbed herself until pleasure mounted. Then she plunged her fingers into her pussy.

Tension built. Her body ached. She sobbed and rubbed harder.

Her thighs tightened. She thrust deeper and faster and then she exploded, her body jackknifing into a maelstrom of pleasure.

JJ awoke with a strangled gasp. Her heart crashed against her chest. Her quilts were tangled around her thighs and her hand was nestled between her trembling thighs.

Her pussy felt wet. Her body strained for release.

The room was empty. No naked cowboys. It had been a dream. Such a vivid, naughty fantasy. The ache of wanting them fucking her threaded through with an intense need. Her body ached and her clit pulsed beneath her fingers.

Aside from her heavy breathing, icy snow and wind blew against the dark windows. But inside the house, an eerie quietness hung in the air. No fire flickered in the fireplace and the battery-operated alarm clock ticked softly on her night table. Four fifty-nine. The alarm clock would go off in one minute.

She blew out a tense breath, reached out and turned off the alarm before it could shatter the quiet. Then she flicked on the bedside lamp. Nothing happened.

Crap, still no electricity. Brady would be putting on the generators soon. A hot shower would have to wait until the generator warmed the water tank.

Her cheeks heated and sexual frustration gnawed through her as she suddenly wished her dream was reality, but she knew something so scandalous was better left to her imagination.

From somewhere she heard a rumble of an engine, and a second later, the light came on. Brady was up. The other guys would be climbing out of bed soon. They would be hungry.

With a groan, she untangled her quilts and climbed out of bed.

The week passed quickly and JJ loved her duties. The storm dropped so much snow that the ranch looked like a gingerbread house dumped with powdered sugar. The men spent most of the days out of the ranch house in the barn or out with the cattle. When they came in for meals, they ate like hungry wolves. With the help of some recipe books she'd found in one of the drawers, she'd whipped up simple yet nutritious meals.

She was just removing a raspberry pound cake from the oven when, to her surprise, the phone rang from somewhere in the living room. She found a landline tucked beneath a clipboard on an end table.

"Moose Ranch, JJ speaking. How can I help you?" She might as well sound professional. This ranch was, after all, a business.

""JJ. Great to hear your voice. How are you doing? I missed a couple of calls from you." Immediately JJ tensed at her parole officer's stern voice. Her spirits plummeted.

"I'm fine," she said stiffly. She'd grown to hate people in authority. They did bad things and got away with it. Just like her cop stepfather had gotten away with things. Like beating on her mother. The few times her or her mom had called 911 for help, his police buddies would show up, remove him from the house and he'd be back a few hours later, madder than before he'd left. After awhile they'd both been too afraid to ask for help.

"I've been trying to get through, but I heard there was a storm your way that took out your lines."

"We just got the electricity back this morning." Piss off and let me live my life in peace. She'd been doing great, pretending she hadn't just spent the last ten years of her life incarcerated. Now this woman had to crash right through her newfound peace.

An awkward silence followed. She wished she had the nerve to hang up and never have to answer to anyone ever again. But if she did cut this woman off, she would probably send in the SWAT team.

"Do you need help with anything? Are there any problems you'd like to discuss concerning your job?"

"Nope."

"Are your bosses treating you well?"

JJ smiled into the phone. She wondered if perky Sabrina Heathers would faint dead away if JJ told her that she was having wicked ménage dreams about her three cowboys. She didn't have to tell her that she was only fantasizing, but boy oh boy did she wish it were true.

"They are perfect gentlemen. I couldn't ask for better bosses." It was true. The three guys were such sweethearts.

She swore she could hear Sabrina smiling over the phone. If that were even possible, to hear someone smile.

"Any panic attacks?"

"None." This perfect place had cured her.

"Wonderful. So, you're taking your meds, then?"

"No meds needed." Gosh, she was so damned nosy.

"Perfect. Can I speak to one of your employers?"

It was exactly at that moment that Brady stepped into the kitchen. Gosh, she hadn't even heard him coming in from outside.

"Yeah, just a minute. One of them just walked in."

Tension zipped through her as she held up the phone and motioned Brady to come into the living room. Embarrassment heated her face.

"My parole officer wants to talk to you."

Brady didn't show any emotion as he took the phone. She wished she could stay and listen, but it would be rude. Besides, she needed to get lunch on the table. Her guys were hungry after tending to their cattle and doing chores.

"Hello, sorry we haven't been in touch. The phone lines were down. What can I do for you?" Brady's strong voice echoed through the room and whispered over her nerve endings, bringing that unique awareness of him cascading over her whenever he was around.

Keeping one ear on the conversation while she quickly prepared roast beef sandwiches and stacked them on a plate, she grinned at his answers. From what Brady was telling Sabrina, it appeared as if all the guys liked her and she was working out better than they had ever imagined.

Yes, she was a conscientious worker and a fast learner and she was fitting in. Yes, the phones and power had gone out and just been restored earlier this morning.

Wow! Her parole officer was asking Brady so many questions it seemed like she wanted to find out if JJ had done something wrong. That would give the authorities an excuse to come and get her, take her back to prison, lock her up and have full control over her again, just like her stepfather had had over her. She felt safe here. She didn't want to go back there. She absolutely loved taking care of these guys.

She hadn't realized her nerves were strung too tightly until her heart began to pound frantically and the familiar urge to run away screaming hit her like a giant truck. It was the same terrifying panic she experienced as when she'd been locked in a cell or in that damn basement closet.

No escape. No control.

She'd forgotten how violent these sensations could be. The feeling of panic came right out of the blue. The kitchen walls began to waver and close in around her. Restlessness made her tummy queasy and she couldn't catch her breath. The room was stifling.

Oh gosh, she was going to die. She needed to get out of here.

"JJ? What's wrong?" Brady's deep voice crashed through her frantic thoughts. He'd already hung up the phone and had walked into the kitchen. She hadn't even realized it until he grabbed her hands and held them tight.

She shook her head. Anxiety swelled inside of her.

Oh God, she was going to die.

"You look scared. Are you having one of those attacks?"

"Yes." *How embarrassing.*

Dan and Rafe were here now too. When had they come in?

"Just breathe. Deep and slow." Dan's voice was soothing as she followed it back to feeling halfway normal.

"Where are your meds?" Rafe asked. His concerned face hovered right in front of her.

"My room, but I don't want to take one." Oh damn. If she took her meds, she'd zone out and be useless for the rest of the day.

"I'll go and get them," Rafe said and he was gone.

"Don't look so devastated," Brady said in what she perceived as a false cheeriness.

"I'm sorry. I don't want to be a bother."

She felt terrible. This was simply awful and she'd been doing so well. Would she ever feel normal? Her heart hammered in her ears and her hands shook in Brady's grip. She felt like screaming and running.

Focus on your breathing. The rest will follow.

"She's been cooped up in here for too long. She needs fresh air." Rafe was back. Gosh, he moved fast.

"Sit down, JJ. Drink some water," Dan instructed. Brady helped her sit and then he let go of her hands. She felt abandoned.

Her hands shook as she accepted a glass of water from Brady but she refused the drug from Rafe.

"I'm fine. Just give me a few minutes."

To her surprise, she was beginning to think a bit more clearly now that she'd focused on controlling her breathing. Adrenaline continued to whip through her body and her hands continued to tremble.

"What the hell happened to trigger this?" Dan snapped.

"I was on the phone with her parole officer and she just started looking wild-eyed," Brady explained.

"Damn it. I forgot that we needed to keep in touch with them," Rafe growled.

"Get her dressed warm. We're going out to get that Christmas tree." Brady's excitement shot through some of her anxiety.

Christmas tree. Yes, this would be a good distraction.

"But you guys need to eat your lunch."

"We'll eat when we get back. You're already looking better. I'll get the snowmobiles running," Brady said.

The men moved quickly.

Rafe and Dan hovered around her like two mother hens, helping her get dressed into appropriate winter wear. By the time she was wrapped snugly in her winter parka, hat, mittens and boots, her panic had eased and Brady had three bright-yellow snowmobiles purring and waiting for them just outside the mudroom. One of the machines had a long metal sled hitched to the back.

"Whooee!" Dan yelled as he popped open the door and led JJ outside.

The icy cold air blasted against her face, sucking the breath right out of her lungs. But the chilled air was just what she needed. It was beautiful out here. Sunshine glistened like jewels on the snow and she felt as if she were standing in a snow village with the barn, fences and sheds covered in white.

To her surprise, she was feeling pretty darned good too. Distraction about getting the Christmas tree had pushed away the anxiety that stupid phone call had caused. Heading outside was just what she needed.

She was finally getting her Christmas tree!

Chapter Five

"That one!" JJ squealed from immediately behind Dan and he automatically slowed his snowmobile. Up until now JJ had been quietly sitting on the padded bench seat behind him with her arms wrapped tightly around his waist and her cheek nestled against his shoulder as he followed the tracks that Rafe and Brady had blazed with their machines.

He followed his gaze to where she pointed up ahead and to the left. The lone pine tree sat in a large clearing.

And the pine tree was huge.

No sooner had he turned off the ignition and JJ had scrambled off the snowmobile and immediately sank up to her knees in the white powder. She'd already removed her helmet and goggles and surprise washed over her features.

"Oh my gosh! I didn't know snow got this deep!" she laughed.

"This is nothing. Wait until January and February. It will be past your hips."

To his surprise, she began struggling toward the what he estimated as a good eight-foot-tall blue spruce about fifteen feet off the track.

Damn fine-looking tree, he had to admit. He just didn't feel much like getting his pants wet wading through all that snow. It was a good thing Brady had packed a couple of snowshoes for them, along with a saw, in the back of the trailer.

He wanted to call out to JJ and get her to return, but she was already at the tree. Within a minute, he had his snowshoes strapped to his boots, an extra pair of snowshoes for JJ strapped to his back, and the handsaw clutched in his hand.

When he met her at the tree, her eyes twinkled merrily and her cheeks were flushed red from the cold.

She looked really pretty and sexy and sweet as she stared up at the tree.

"I don't know if this is such a nice tree. It's kind of scrawny. Here, look at the bald spot right there." He pointed to a nonexistent bald spot and enjoyed it when she shook her head and smiled at him.

"Quit kidding and quit stalling. This is our tree. Cut," she ordered.

"At your service. But put on these snowshoes so you'll have an easier trek back."

He handed her the wood webbed items. She shook her head and laughed as she grabbed the snowshoes and peered at them.

"I've never been on a pair in my life."

Curiosity won out and he grinned as she placed them on the snow in front of her.

"I am not about to get on those funny-looking contraptions. They don't even match my attire."

Dan blinked in shock. *Didn't match her attire*? Was she a fashionista? Did they even make designer snowshoes?

To his surprise, she burst out laughing. The sound was so sweet that his breath literally backed up into his lungs.

"You should see your face. Got you back!" she laughed.

Man, she was so beautiful when she laughed. So not city girl, but not country girl either.

He shook his head. Not city. Not country. What the hell was he thinking? He set about scooping snow away from the base of the tree, then placed the saw against the bark and began to cut.

JJ wished for a digital camera as she watched Dan cutting the tree. It was going to look so beautiful in the living room. She already had the spot picked out. Right beside the fireplace and in front of the living room window.

Dan looked sexy in his winter hat and the dark shadow lining his red cheeks and chin. He was such a cheerful guy and she loved being around him. She could have gotten some really good shots with a camera of all three of them...something to remember them by, if something happened where she'd get sent back to prison. Sadness swooped in around her and she frowned. Why would this last? In her life whenever she got happy, something bad happened. Why would this time be any different?

"Timber!" Dan's yell crashed through her thoughts as he took a couple of steps back. A large crack ripped through the air. The tree swayed and then fell in slow motion away from them. It hit the powdery snow with a big puff.

"I'll get it on the trailer and we can wait for the guys to circle back when they realize we aren't following," Dan said. "You strap on those snowshoes and I'll give you a quick lesson. A girl living out here needs to know how to walk in snowshoes."

She wrinkled her nose as she stared at the shoes. She wanted to ask Dan exactly how to put them on, but he'd already grabbed the tree, hoisted it up over his shoulder and was heading back to their snowmobile.

He did make it look easy as he barely sank into the snow. He was practically walking on snow and she was knee-deep in it and her feet were getting wet and cold from the snow that had fallen in her boots and melted. It wasn't very comfortable.

"How in the world do I put these on?" She called to Dan after he placed the tree on the sled. She wasn't even sure the sled would be able to transport the tree, for the sled was hidden somewhere beneath all those pine branches.

"Be right there!"

She had to admit she was impressed with how easily he walked in the snowshoes.

"First, you place the snowshoes near your feet," he said a moment later when he returned. "Then you place a foot into one shoe. Here, I'll hold you and then you can do it."

His arm snuggled around her waist and he held her firm. His scent was pleasant, a combination of soap and a tinge of aftershave. She liked it.

"There you go," he said quietly as she placed one booted foot onto one snowshoe. While holding her steady with one arm, he leaned down and strapped on the boot. Then he straightened.

"And now the other foot," he instructed.

She struggled as she lifted her other foot out of the deep snow, but thankfully he kept holding her. He strapped the other boot and she was standing on top of the snow, instead of in it.

It was an amazing feeling.

"I guess I should have waited until we had snowshoes on before leaving the snowmobile," she said with a laugh.

"I guess so," he muttered. He was still holding onto her and she ventured a step forward.

The webbed contraption on her feet felt awkward.

"Keep your legs far enough apart so you can walk without the edges of the snowshoes touching each other," he coached.

She nodded and took another step forward. Then another.

He kept pace with her, his body pressing against hers as he held her waist. Hmm, he felt very nice as his hip rubbed against hers and suddenly she couldn't concentrate on walking. Instead she began to wonder how he would come over her naked body, his long thick shaft thrusting deep into her pussy.

Mercy! He was making her way too warm for comfort.

"Okay, let me try on my own." To her surprise her voice sounded breathy and husky.

She needed to get a bit away from him so she could focus on the snowshoeing and not on him.

He did as she asked and she took a step forward. Something prevented her one foot from moving and suddenly she was airborne. A second later she met the powdery cold snow face on.

Behind her, Dan cursed softly. Then strong hands grabbed her around the waist and she was flying through the air again like a ragdoll. A second later he had her standing.

"Sweet mercy, but you are strong!" she whispered as she brushed snow off her cheeks and eyelashes.

To her surprise, he began to laugh.

"You look like one of those white snow bunnies."

I do?

She gazed down at herself. Yep, snow clung to her jeans, her coat and, well, everywhere. She grimaced as some wet snow slipped past her collar and dripped down her back. Man, that was cold!

"You've got a white beard and white eyebrows. You look like Santa!" He managed to say as he kept laughing.

Hmm, white beard and white eyebrows, did she? She looked like Santa Claus?

She resisted the urge to push him into the snow and start laughing. That would be so childish, and yet...

With one quick push to his chest, he was sailing through the air. He landed on his back with a plop. Powdery snow puffed up from his sides and the surprised expression on his face was priceless.

He began to laugh again.

Warmth and joy bubbled and something cold and hard that she hadn't even realized was buried deep inside her heart suddenly broke off and melted away. His laughter was contagious and happiness swept through her in such a huge overwhelming wave that suddenly it was very easy to crack a genuine grin. It felt good. Really good.

"Come on! Help me up!" He held out his gloved hands.

She hobbled over to him, thrilled that she wasn't falling over her snowshoes. She reached out and grabbed his hands. His grip was firm and without warning he gave her a powerful yank. She screeched as she lost her balance.

This time instead of falling into the snow, she fell right on top of Dan! Her body aligned perfectly over his length and her face was inches from his. Suddenly a sobering look caressed his face. He stopped laughing the moment his erection pushed against the juncture of her thighs.

Oh my. Having his hard body beneath hers was nice.

"Oops," he whispered.

His eyes were a dreamy green and matched the surrounding pine trees. And his eyelashes were black and so long. He blinked and she noticed his eyes darken as his cock continued to grow beneath her.

Her breath went kind of funny in her chest as his lips slightly parted. His hands settled on her hips. They were strong and confident, his palms hot. Suddenly she wanted to know how it would feel having his mouth moving against hers. Before she knew what she was doing, she lowered her head. She closed her eyes.

His breath was warm as it caressed her lips. A sweet tremor burst through her as her mouth melted over his. His scent invaded her senses and his lips were firm and demanding, making every nerve ending in her body zing to life. As he pushed his tongue into her mouth, a shock of pleasure burst through her. Her tongue tangled with his and a sharp pang of need pooled deep inside her pussy.

A guttural sound from somewhere deep inside her chest echoed through the cold air. He kissed her harder and desire rocked her. Shivery sensations moved up her inner thighs and her legs tightened. She pressed her lower belly against his thick arousal and a thousand pleasure vibrations twisted around her. Heat whipped through her much in the same way as when she dreamed about them.

From somewhere far off, she could hear the purring engines from the snowmobiles, warning her that Brady and Rafe were driving closer. She knew she should stop kissing Dan, but he made her feel wonderfully heady and as aroused as she had during that kiss she'd shared with Brady that first night she'd arrived.

The hum of the vehicles grew louder, but she just didn't care if Brady and Rafe found them like this.

She gyrated her hips against Dan's leg, loving the incredible pleasure bursting inside her.

Suddenly Dan broke the kiss on a groan.

"We have to stop," he whispered against her mouth.

Stop? She didn't want to stop. She wanted to keep going. She was about to press her mouth against his again, but Brady's shout stopped her cold.

"Hey you two! You should take all that arm and leg tangling indoors or you'll freeze your asses out here before too long."

Mercy! She hadn't realized they were right here! She turned her head to find both Brady and Rafe sitting astride their snowmobiles not more than twenty feet away from them.

Despair shot through her. She expected to be admonished for her behavior, but neither of the men seemed angry. Instead, teasing glints twinkled in their eyes and sweet smiles lifted their lips. They actually looked as if they were enjoying themselves watching them kissing in the snow.

Dan didn't seem embarrassed or mad either as he licked his lips. "I hope there's plenty more where that came from." He didn't wait for an answer. He winked and angled her to the side of his body and managed to stand very quickly. He held out his hands and she grabbed them.

He hoisted her to her feet with ease.

"Nice-looking tree," Rafe complimented as they neared the snowmobile.

"JJ picked it." Dan replied.

Brady nodded and said nothing as Dan untied her snowshoes and then his own. But she could feel the heat of Rafe and Brady's gazes as they watched her straddle the padded bench seat. Suddenly she had the inkling that their perceptions about her had changed. She wasn't exactly sure why she had that instinct, but she possessed an intriguing awareness about them now. Before, she'd managed to contain it to her dreams and fantasies, but she couldn't do it anymore.

Theirs was not an employee-employer relationship anymore. Not even friends. Something deeper, darker and very sexual was brewing inside of her. Brady's kiss that first night had unleashed it, and now Dan's kiss had ignited it.

Those naughty ménage fantasies she'd been having suddenly seemed a lot closer to reality. But JJ wasn't sure what she should do about it.

Rafe noted JJ had been unusually quiet since they'd returned with the tree. Sure, outwardly she seemed happy that the tree fit perfectly where she wanted it to go. She'd acted like an excited kid when they'd all pitched in to hang the ornaments and then the Christmas lights.

She'd even talked them into popping popcorn as they wolfed down their sandwiches and drank coffee while she started preparing supper. Then they'd strung the popcorn onto strings and hung them on the tree. Afterward, she'd gotten kind of quiet again.

He wondered if maybe she was worried that she might have another panic attack—or perhaps she was shy because Brady and he had caught them kissing.

Actually, he'd enjoyed watching Dan and her in the snow. Brady, it appeared, had also been enthralled. He hadn't been able to keep his eyes off JJ since they'd come back. Hell, none of them could keep their eyes off her. She was like a beautiful fire and they knew they shouldn't touch her because they would get burned.

Since that kiss with Dan, he sensed the easygoing relationship between all of them had changed. He didn't know if it had transformed for the better, or if what was now blossoming between all of them was fragile. Would things would fall apart if the three of them decided to take her to the next level?

"I swear it is the most beautiful tree I have ever seen," JJ whispered as she set a bowl full of mashed potatoes on the dining table then sat between Rafe and Brady. She simply could not get enough of looking at it. The ornaments Jenna had sent were so cute. They weren't the cheap plastic ornaments, like they had in prison. These were the traditional fragile glass ones that she remembered from when she'd been a kid. The colorful ones that shattered if you dropped them.

There were angels, frosted pine cones and round ones with designs. Traditional colors of green, red and gold. Everything matched so beautifully. Everything glittered and her heart just about burst with happiness as she kept staring at the tree.

Spoons clattered as the guys helped themselves to the mashed potatoes, beef steaks, applesauce and vegetables she'd whipped up for them. She ignored them and just stared at the tree. If she tried hard enough she could almost hear her mother calling out her name, telling JJ Santa had come and left her a present. Could almost see her standing in front of the tree in her slippers and robe, her heart-shaped face glowing as she smiled and picked up the lone present.

Then she'd turn to JJ and envelope her in a hug and kiss before finally handing her her gift.

"Merry Christmas, sweet pea," she'd say softly. So softly. So tenderly.

"I would think Christmas is pretty tough being away from your family," Brady suddenly said as he scooped the last of the mashed potatoes onto his plate.

Brady's comment made her frown. Made her remember how fun it had been when she'd been a kid and it had just been her mom and herself. Christmas had been so normal. Because they'd been poor, she'd received one present each Christmas, but that had been so exciting.

She missed her mom. She wished her mother could have met these guys. She would have loved them immediately.

JJ frowned as sadness swept over her.

"What's wrong?" Rafe's concerned voice crashed through her melancholy.

She shook her head and forced a smile as the three men stared at her with worry. Oh crap! She was ruining their evening and that was the last thing she wanted to do.

"Just remembering things," she replied.

She hoped that Brady would get the hint that she didn't want to talk about her past. She grabbed the empty bowls and stood.

"Anyone for more?" she asked.

A loud round of affirmation for potatoes but not vegetables had happiness whipping through her again. She hoped the thread of her past would drop, so she stayed a little extra longer at the counter scooping the potatoes into the bowl.

When she returned, the guys quieted and stared at her.

"If you want to call your family, that's not a problem," Brady said.

"I don't have any family." It was an automatic response. She'd gotten used to saying it over the years to the incoming inmates who asked. Usually they dropped the subject, but Brady was like a dog with a bone.

"Everybody has family. I've got a crazy sister who loves matchmaking all our siblings. There's eight of us. And Dan has two sisters and Rafe has two adopted brothers and two adopted sisters plus he had a house full of foster siblings over the years. You have no brothers or sisters?" Brady asked.

"None that I know of," she said. She placed the bowl onto the table and reluctantly sat down. It appeared the men were very curious about her and it was time to come clean.

"Parents?" Rafe prodded.

She shook her head. "Dead."

"Aunts, uncles, grandparents?" Dan asked.

"Nope, just me."

The guys looked at each other with perplexed expressions on their faces. It was obvious that they could not comprehend that she had no one.

"Wow, I sure know how to kill a conversation, don't I? It's why I've been avoiding talking about my past."

"We've noticed," Rafe said softly.

Since she had been here, they had asked, but she'd always managed to deflect their questions and change the subject. Today, she hadn't been able to. Perhaps that panic attack had weakened her resolve.

Despite the sorrow clutching her heart, she managed a bright smile. She was like that—the gloomier she got inside, the cheerier she tried to be outside. It was a coping mechanism. She couldn't stand people feeling sorry for her.

"Well then, you'll have to consider us your family, right boys?" Dan said with a huge grin.

The other two men vehemently agreed.

"And we come with a lot of family. They drop in unexpectedly all the time," Rafe chuckled.

"Last year, Brady's sister, Jenna, who is the oldest of all eight, dropped in here over the holidays . It was the first time she'd been able to make it out this way, right, Brady? Anyway, we call Jenna the matchmaking one for his family. She's always trying to find the perfect mate for her siblings. So far, she has been unsuccessful," Rafe said.

"She did not approve of the fact we had no Christmas tree," Brady said with a laugh.

"Hence the ornaments," JJ added. "I love your sister already."

"You should. Without her, we wouldn't have you," Dan said with a soft voice that melted like delicious chocolate over her senses.

"How do you mean?"

"She runs an employment agency and has contracts with the prison system," Rafe stated.

"And we were surprised when you showed up because we were expecting two guys, umpf." A nudge to Dan's belly from Rafe made Dan shut up.

Three bashful faces stared at her.

"You were expecting two men?" *Oh dear.* Now that she thought about it, Brady had stared at her kind of oddly when he'd first found her sitting on her suitcases on the lake. And then he'd been angry. She'd thought it was because she'd been drunk. The guys had looked funny at her too when they'd first met that night. And she suddenly remembered talk about there being a mistake. How in the world had she forgotten that?

"We didn't think to ask if JJ was a man's name. But we did ask for a couple of men," Dan replied.

"But the questionnaire that you filled out for the Freedom Run program was exactly what we were looking for and, come to think of it, didn't say if you were a female or male. I would suspect Jenna had something to do with that," Brady said with a reassuring smile.

"Yeah, your answers to that questionnaire had us sold, sight unseen," Rafe said quickly.

JJ frowned. She wasn't sure if she liked the idea that they hadn't been expecting her.

"So you guys like drunk and drugged women then?"

The men didn't say anything. Their looks were uneasy. It appeared they hadn't wanted her to know she'd been sent here by mistake.

"Hey, sweetheart, don't be sad. You had me the first minute I saw you," Rafe said tenderly.

"You had me the minute I tasted your chocolate pudding," Dan said with a wink.

"Ah, the way to a man's heart is through his eyes and stomach," she joked.

The two men turned to Brady. She followed their gazes to Brady, suddenly eager to hear what he had to say.

Brady crossed his arms in front of his chest and shifted uncomfortably on his chair. His face possessed that same shyness that she'd noticed that first night when she'd been drunk and asked him to put on his cowboy hat.

"Oh, come on, Brady. Tell us. When did JJ have you?" Dan prodded.

Brady looked directly at JJ and her tummy flip-flopped wonderfully at his heated look.

"She had me at our first kiss," he said.

Oh.

Heat blasted into her cheeks. Excited whistles erupted from Dan and Rafe.

"What? Rafe guffawed.

"And here I thought I was the only lucky guy who got a kiss." Dan shook his head with what she hoped was mock anger on his face. He clutched a fist to his heart.

"Hell, I'm the one who should be pissed off," Rafe complained. "I haven't even been kissed."

"I'll kiss you," Dan said and smacked his lips together, making a squeaking sound.

"Get out of here." Rafe rolled his eyes and laughed.

"Maybe I should kiss you, Rafe. So you don't feel left out?" JJ teased.

"Pucker up, my man. She kisses real nice," Dan chuckled and slapped Rafe's back.

A burst of self-consciousness bit into her as all three men suddenly focused their attention on her, their gazes expectant. Goodness, she had just been teasing them.

They really wanted her to kiss Rafe? She looked at Brady and caught herself. Why should she care what he thought? And why did she suddenly want his approval?

To her surprise, he gave her a nod. He wanted her to kiss Rafe. She could tell by that same intense look of interest he'd displayed when he'd caught her kissing Dan.

Dan watched her keenly. She gazed at Rafe. His expectant smile created some wonderful trembles inside her lower belly. Suddenly, the idea of kissing Rafe in front of the other two men was a real turn-on.

She stood and Brady and Dan cheered.

"Oh, Rafe! Looks as if you are gonna get your kiss," Dan said with a grin. Arousal flared in his green eyes.

Brady settled back in his chair and folded his arms casually across his chest. His blue eyes were dark and intense as he studied her.

Heat swirled low in her belly.

"It's because she's saved the best for last," Rafe replied with a wink.

JJ's heart hammered crazily as she walked around her chair and stood in front of Rafe. His brown eyes dilated with sexual hunger. Something lusty whipped through her. Her breathing quickened and hot blood coursed through her veins.

Suddenly, he reached out and grabbed her around the waist. She let out a yelp as he pulled her onto his lap.

Instantly she felt the hard length of his arousal pressing against her pussy and ass. Liquid heat tore through her as she suddenly had a vision of Rafe undressing her and then the men taking turns making love to her right up against the kitchen counter.

Intense warmth burned into her cheeks. She shouldn't be thinking such thoughts. It was inappropriate and yet...

"I've been waiting for this kiss for a long time," Rafe whispered. His voice sounded so tender, and her instincts told her that he would be an attentive lover.

"Come on, JJ, kiss him," Dan whispered.

Excitement swirled around her. Rafe was suddenly a magnet. Her lips tingled. She wanted his sexy mouth. Wanted to feel his lips on hers. Just one kiss. Just to see what could have been.

She lowered her head and closed her eyes. Her lips melted over his.

Sensations swamped her. She lifted her hands and splayed them over his warm chest. His heart pounded against her palms. One of his hands slipped into her hair and he pressed his palm against the back of her head, bringing her deeper into the kiss.

His tongue forced her lips apart and she slanted her mouth harder against his. Her skin felt sizzling. His scent turned her on. He smelled so good. Like dark forests and fresh air and happiness.

Suddenly, she wanted his hands touching her. Wanted him to push her down onto the table and start fucking her.

His kiss became more forceful. She whimpered as arousal flooded her. His cock jerked and swelled beneath her. His erection was huge and the friction of it pushing against her pussy was doing awesome things to her insides.

"She kisses really nice," Rafe said as he suddenly broke the kiss. He was breathing hard. She was breathing harder.

A tingly headiness had her almost toppling off his lap, but Rafe's arms tightened around her. Whew! The man sure did know how to kiss!

"Wow, you are one Romeo, Rafe. You've knocked her off her feet," Dan laughed.

"All right, boys, I think we'd better call this a night before things get out of hand," Brady said in a rough voice.

She didn't dare look at him, for if she did she knew the hot look on his face would make her want to do some more naughty things, things that she should not be doing with her employers.

"Take the rest of the night off, JJ. It's been quite an eventful day for us. We'll finish off things down here."

JJ nodded and reluctantly climbed off Rafe's lap.

Have mercy! What had she just done? And why did she want to do so much more? With all three of them!

Chapter Six

Brady had remained relatively silent as the three of them removed the dishes from the table, washed them and put them away. Today had been an interesting day, to say the least.

First, with JJ's anxiety attack while he'd been on the phone with her parole officer, and then Dan kissing her. Spying on her while she was in the arms of another man had turned him on. Big time. Then, while watching her kiss Rafe, his cock had swelled and he'd fantasized about fucking her right there on top of the dining table.

Since JJ had gone upstairs, Dan and Rafe were acting jovial as if nothing had happened with JJ. But, they'd always been pretty good at covering their true emotions. Him, not so much.

Due to their schedule being interrupted this afternoon, they knew they would be up quite late tending to the cattle and doing other chores. It wouldn't be until past midnight when all of them would climb into their beds. But only then would he be able to claim some semblance of peace in the privacy of his own bedroom.

His shaft was as hard as a spike and he needed relief. But only the kind that JJ could give him. In the meantime, he needed to figure out how to proceed with their relationship.

She'd been excited about kissing Rafe. He'd seen it in her eyes as she'd looked to him for approval. He'd given it and watching the two of them kissing had really excited him. Dan too, had shifted uncomfortably in his chair, probably making room for his engorged erection pressing against his pants.

It wouldn't be the first time they'd shared a woman who all three of them were interested in. But those other women were different. He'd known they would move on after they'd left. They were temporary.

With JJ, he had the feeling things were going to be permanent. Now, all he had to do was figure out if she was receptive to having sex with all of them. Separately and together.

Two more weeks until Christmas, JJ thought as she slipped into the steamy shower stall. She wasn't sure how long masturbating under the sounds of running water was going to keep the sexual edge off. There was only so long one woman who'd been in prison for so long could handle her sexual urges around three sexy cowboys—who, to her disappointment, didn't wear cowboy hats...except in her fantasies and dreams.

Since that day she'd kissed Rafe and Dan, the dynamics of the easygoing employee-employer relationship had changed. She'd become conscious of their heated looks and quite aware of her own reactions to the men.

She'd begun to fantasize about them during the day while she went about doing her housework, while preparing their meals as well as when she stepped into the shower.

JJ blew out a tense breath as hot water pummelled her shoulder muscles. Nervous energy made her eager to masturbate and take off the sexual edge, so she immediately grabbed the scented soap and began to lather her body. She soaped her throat and down her sides, then paid special attention to her breasts, lathering her nipples.

Sensuously, she rubbed them and tugged her nipples until they turned hard and achy and her lower belly tightened. Leaving one hand to massage her breasts, she slid the bar of soap lower and slowly soaped her belly. She widened her legs and slipped the bar between her thighs and slid the slippery soap back and forth over her clitoris.

Her breathing quickened. Her legs tightened.

Her hand massaged first one and then her other breast, her fingers continuously rubbing her tender wet nipples.

She moved the foamy soap bar faster and faster.

She shuddered and gasped. Her pussy clenched, demanding penetration. Lifting one leg, she placed her foot onto the edge of the bathtub, spreading her legs wider. She rubbed the slippery bar faster and faster over her wet clit and moaned softly as her vaginal muscles clenched.

She imagined the three men slipping into the shower to be with her. Water sluicing over their tanned muscles. Their cocks, erect and swollen, ready to pleasure her.

Two of them would move in front of her, their heads lowering. Two mouths lapping at her nipples. Another man dropping onto his knees in front of her, his hot mouth melting over her clitoris. He would suck hard.

Pleasure explode through her. She gyrated her hips and rode the agonizing waves, rubbing the bar of soap harder and harder.

For a few tumultuous seconds she didn't care if they heard her. Let them hear. She dropped the soap and thrust three fingers into her pussy. Her muscles eagerly clenched them and she cried out as she came.

"I told you," Rafe whispered.

He, Brady and Dan listened to the rush of water coming from JJ's bathroom. They stood right outside her bathroom door and every few seconds a sultry moan vibrated above the shower stream.

Beside him Dan cursed softly and Brady clenched his jaw. Fire lanced their eyes. Rafe recognized their looks. He felt the intoxicating need for release shooting through his system as well.

Lately, he'd been hearing sexy mews, but at first he'd thought it was just wishful thinking.

Rafe blew out a tense breath as she moaned again. This time a bit louder.

"Maybe she wants us to hear?" Dan suggested.

"Well, if she does, then we've heard," Brady replied gruffly.

"Does anyone have any ideas of what we can do to help alleviate her sexual tension?" Rafe asked. He wasn't sure how long he could stay here listening to her sultry moans every morning and every night when she showered.

"I have an idea," Brady said softly.

With a nod of his head, he indicated they should move away from the bathroom door and leave her bedroom.

JJ was just removing the third of three bread pans from the oven when she thought she heard the low rumble of an airplane. Normally a plane passing overhead didn't bother her, but this one sounded different. It was close and in the general direction of the lake.

She peeked out the kitchen window and noticed a pitch-black bush plane coming to a halt on the frozen lake. The plane was similar in size to the one she'd arrived in.

A prickle of uneasiness zipped through her as she watched Brady stroll down the trail to the plane. One person, a pretty auburn-haired woman wearing a powder-blue ski jacket and pants, climbed out of the plane. She shook hands with Brady.

They conversed for several minutes before she disappeared into the plane again and a moment later she handed Brady a medium-sized cardboard box, which he placed on the ice. She handed him a second box, this one smaller, and he put it on top of the other one.

They waved to each other and then the plane roared off again.

She watched as Brady carried one of the boxes up the trail and into the barn. Minutes later he strolled down to the lake and retrieved the second box, strolled back up and disappeared into the barn with it.

Huh, she hadn't known he'd ordered something for ranch use. She could have used some properly fitting clothes. All this ranch life and healthy eating was making her curvier in some places, especially her breasts.

She grinned to herself. She'd been here almost a month and she hadn't even thought about taking off and disappearing like she'd wanted to do when she'd been told she was getting a job out here. She'd also managed not to have any more full-blown panic attacks during her short conversations with her parole officer. But speaking with the woman continued to make her anxious, despite Sabrina being polite and cheerful. She didn't like feeling uncomfortable with authority figures. It kind of ruined her day. She just wished she knew what to do about it.

The mouthwatering scent of her freshly baked bread grabbed her attention and ripped her back to reality. The guys would be here for supper in less than an hour and she needed to hurry to get the rest of dinner ready.

Excitement bubbled through her as she thought about the possibilities of expanding her cooking abilities by ordering a couple more recipe books over the Internet. Until now, she'd stayed away from the computer. The guys had shown her how to use it one night, along with which stores they used to order supplies and how to contact North Country Air for the delivery.

Gosh, she'd had no idea she'd love cooking and baking so much. Or that she'd so quickly fall in love with those men. It warmed her heart when she watched them eating the food she prepared for them. They said she should consider them family. She considered them much more than that. Loving them was a dream. A dream she hoped she would never wake up from, because she knew in reality she could never have a happily-ever-after with all three of them.

Three hours later, JJ stepped out of her bathroom and into her bedroom. She was tired from a full day's work. She'd prepared three square meals for her men, cleaned and dusted a good portion of the living room and all the bathrooms. She'd even managed to get in some snowshoe practice behind the house. Since Dan had shown her how to snowshoe, she'd been practicing outside every morning for about half an hour.

The air was always fresh and icy cold, but it perked up her senses for the day. While she'd been in prison she'd seriously missed the snow. Winters had been brutal and she'd never had proper winter clothing to keep her warm and they'd always plowed the snow from the yards, piling it in ugly heaps.

Besides, with her frequent panic attacks, she'd been inside more than out. Heck, they'd even nicknamed her Panic in the prison infirmary.

She was glad to be out of there. So happy to be here.

As she passed one of her bedroom windows she smiled at the snowflakes whirling against the windowpane. It was snowing again. They'd have a white Christmas for sure. She removed her towel and tossed it on the bed.

And froze with surprise.

A small package sat on her bed. It was wrapped in red-and-green-striped Christmas paper.

How delightful! One of the guys had gotten her an early Christmas present.

She picked up the envelope beside the present and opened it. A cute card with a snowman in a meadow.

JJ,

If you chose to accept this present, please leave the empty wrapper on the dining room table tomorrow morning.

Brady, Dan and *Rafe*

What did they mean if she chose to accept this present?

In a moment she had the box unwrapped and her mouth dropped open with surprise. Three different sizes of butt plugs sat in an unopened package. All three were shaped like Christmas trees. Bright green with a wide bases, tapering toward the top.

Oh my goodness!

She swallowed and bit her bottom lip. Did this mean...all three of them wanted to have sex with her? All their names were on the card. It had to mean all three of them.

She had to be dreaming. She had to be nuts, even to be considering doing it!

Stunned at this unexpected turn of events, she didn't know how long she stared at the package before she opened it. The instructions made her catch her breath. She'd never worn a butt plug before, but it appeared the three men wanted to make her secret fantasies come true! What in the world was she going to do?

"Does anyone want any more bacon and eggs?" JJ called out from where she stood at the stove, cracking several more eggs into the frying pan.

No replies. She grinned, despite the mixed emotions of nervousness and excitement whirling through her. They always went for a second round of breakfast, but she knew why there were quiet this morning. It had everything to do with the empty butt plug package she'd left smack-dab in the middle of the dining room table.

"What's the matter? Are all my cowboys sick today? You can't do your work or have play time if you don't have enough energy," she teased.

Despite not wanting for it to happen, her face grew warm.

A chorus of answers for "more food, please" echoed throughout the room.

JJ nodded.

"That's better. More grub coming in just a few minutes. Pour yourselves more coffee."

She didn't have to turn to look as she heard the racket when all three of the men scrambled toward the coffeemaker.

Huh, interesting turn of events. It seemed as if she suddenly had them eating out of her hands. It was amazing what accepting butt plugs could do.

"She was killing me at breakfast," Rafe complained as the three of them tossed packages of vitamin cubes onto the freshly plowed area near the barn. Plump, pregnant Angus cows milled here and there, grabbing their morning breakfast of hay. The cubes they scattered for the cattle helped to bolster the pre-calving cows, whose appetites dropped as their calves grew larger inside them.

They kept the soon-to-calve cows closer to the barn in large corrals. It was easier to keep an eye on them, especially if one had a difficult birth.

"I just about died when I saw that wrapper on the table," Dan chuckled as he ripped open another bag and scattered the vitamin cubes around.

"I just about came," Brady grumbled as he threw another package off the trailer that was attached to the four wheeler he'd used to transport feed to the cattle in the yards.

Rafe and Dan laughed and slapped him on the back. Brady tucked his chin deeper into his coat and grabbed another package. Last night it had snowed, giving a dusting of about three inches, but there was a distinct chill in the air. Colder than usual.

He hadn't checked the weather report on the radio, but he got the feeling winter was finally digging in her heels. Until now, it had continued to be unusually warm at a steady ten degrees below zero Celsius. They would be paying for this milder-than-usual weather soon. For now though he couldn't worry about it.

Life was already difficult enough having a constant hard-on and a massive craving to make love to JJ. He still couldn't believe she'd agreed to the butt plug. Had she been wearing it during breakfast? Or had she waited until they'd left the house before she'd gone to her bathroom to insert it?

Brady groaned as he envisioned her sliding the smallest plug into her tight ass. The package had contained three plugs of varying sizes. She would start with the smallest. It would prepare her for the medium-sized one, until she could use the largest.

Brady blew out his breath. By then her anal muscles would be stretched enough so she could be taken by them. Until then, they had decided they would visit her on a one-on-one basis every night.

Conversation had been quite tense during dinner. JJ had barely been able to breathe as their masculine scents drifted around her in teasing waves while she served lamb chops with baby potatoes and vegetables. Maybe it was the plug nestled snugly in her ass that made her so aware of their every move, their heated looks and their tantalizing smells of sweat and sweet hay.

Whatever it was, it was playing havoc with her senses and making her eager to discover what they were going to do next.

By the time she climbed beneath her flannel sheets, she was ready to do some serious masturbating. She would have brought herself some relief in the shower as she'd done many times already, but the water had turned cold quicker than normal, prompting her to finish in a hurry.

She sighed and switched off her bedside lamp, plunging everything into darkness. Her eyes adjusted quickly and moonlight filtered through the windows illuminating her room with its brightness. She listened impatiently for any sounds indicating that the men were still awake.

But it was unusually quiet tonight. It meant she would have to tame her pleasure so they wouldn't hear.

Unless you let them hear, my dear.

JJ inhaled softly at that idea. Could she tease them like that? Rafe and Dan would hear for sure. It would sent them a message that she wanted sex. With all of them.

She swallowed at that idea. Goodness, she couldn't have sex with all of them, could she? She had been fantasizing about it. But would the reality be as good as the fantasy?

Insecurity bombarded her. Their relationship would change. She really did like all three of them. Their camaraderie with each other was wonderful. Would having sex with all three of them ruin the friendship between the men?

But there was the matter of the butt plugs. All three of them had their names on that card. They knew she wore a plug now. The dynamics of the relationship had changed by her accepting the anal toys. There was no going back.

She pushed the sheets and comforters past her hips, and then closed her eyes. For now she would keep fantasizing and she'd wait for their next move.

Lifting her knees and spreading them apart, she then took a deep breath and glided her hands over her breasts. She loved how smooth and curvy they felt beneath her palms and gasped at the sweet bite of pain as she pulled and twisted her nipples. She took several leisurely moments to play with her nipples and breasts, enjoying the flare of excitement sweeping through her, before gliding her hands downward over her belly.

She slipped a finger between her swollen labia and pressed into her vagina. She was sopping wet because she'd been thinking about the men. Whenever she thought about them, she creamed with anticipation. She withdrew her finger and then tenderly explored every inch of her pussy, stroking and rubbing her clit and labia until arousal swept through her.

Her breaths quickened and she shuddered. She slid her finger into her pussy again and collected warm moisture and withdrew. She massaged harder and harder, moaning as sparks of arousal burst through her. All her inhibitions melted away and she slipped into the pleasure.

Her mind reeled as images of her three cowboys spun through her thoughts. Hard muscles. Taut bodies. Eager mouths kissing her nipples, kissing her belly and licking her pussy.

Sweet shudders wrapped around her. She gyrated and bucked and welcomed the waves of ecstasy. She thrust her fingers repeatedly into her vagina, and rubbed her clit faster and faster, shaking inside the pleasure for as long as she could.

When the pussy spasms slowly ebbed away, JJ smiled.

Wow, that had been an incredible release. Instincts told her that her orgasms would be a hundred times better with her cowboys making love to her.

A soft noise toward her bedroom door made her tense. She opened her eyes and gasped as she caught sight of a silhouette in her bedroom doorway. Whoever stood there wore a cowboy hat.

Oh my gosh! *Brady*?

"Is everything okay?" she asked as she reached down to grab the covers. How embarrassing. How long had he been standing there watching her masturbating?

"Don't." The rough voice belonged to Dan.

She blew out a tense breath and lay back down. She did his bidding and left the covers off, allowing him to see her naked. He remained in the doorway, but she could tell he was also naked. His muscles flexed in the moonlight and a very large and long cock angled up toward his belly.

"Do you understand what the plug means?" he asked in a low voice.

"Yes," she whispered. Her heart began a fast pound.

"Tell me," he instructed.

She shivered as a number of naughty scenarios played through her mind.

"All three of you. Whenever you want." She tossed the last sentence out just to make it clear.

He visibly tensed and for a moment he said nothing.

"And whenever I want," she added.

She couldn't believe she'd just given them verbal permission to have sex with her and she'd also showed them her bold side.

"Tomorrow night, it begins. I will be your first cowboy. We will break you in one at a time."

Break me in.

She nodded jerkily.

He turned and gave her a sweet glimpse of his bare ass.

When he quietly closed the door behind him, she closed her eyes.

Tomorrow night, it begins.

Oh my gosh!

Dan blew out a tense breath as he entered his bedroom. He was so incredibly hard after watching her masturbate that he was going to lose his mind from the tense arousal searing through every inch of him.

She'd looked so hot writhing on the bed with her hips bucking, her legs spread and her hand thrusting between her thighs. He'd been surprised the sheets didn't catch fire. She looked like a dream girl right out of one of those magazines they kept in the barn.

She had curves in all the right places and her breasts would fit right into his palms. Her nipples looked big and erect and her legs were nice and long. He couldn't wait to dive between her thighs and get a taste of her.

She was a beautiful woman, and she belonged to them.

Whenever you want, she'd said. *Whenever I want.*

He hadn't expected her to say those words. He'd expected some shyness, not a bold naked vixen. That JJ was going to accommodate them in the bedroom was amazing. That he was lusting after her with more than just his body, but with his heart also, was surprising.

He pushed back the urge to march right back in there and bring his body over hers and take her tonight. He wanted to make love to her.

But they all were attracted to her and wanted to share her. He would need to stick to their plan and introduce themselves sexually to her one at a time. She had twenty-four hours to get used to the idea that the two of them would be having sex tomorrow night.

Dan reached down between his legs and grabbed his throbbing shaft. Until he met up with JJ tomorrow night, he would have to take the edge off himself.

Chapter Seven

JJ could barely make it through the day. She wanted to say something to Dan about his visit last night. Wanted to tell the guys that she cared deeply for each of them and that she wanted them to remain friends despite this newly forming relationship, but their heated looks just about drove her crazy. It was as if they were all undressing her with their eyes. To tell the truth, she was doing the same to them.

Especially Dan. She'd been fantasizing about him and his big cock and all the yummy muscles she'd spied on him last night. She'd barely slept, tossing and turning while thinking about tonight.

The day dragged on while she did her duties. She cooked and cleaned frantically to keep busy and her mind off tonight.

When she decided to turn in earlier than usual, she called out a goodnight to the men. They acted perfectly normal while seated at the dining room table playing cards. She wasn't sure what she'd expected. Maybe Dan following her up the stairs to her room? Or one of the guys commenting about the way their relationship was turning?

A sharp edge of neediness whispered through her as fifteen minutes later she stepped out of the shower. Things changing so fast, she felt off balance. Everything seemed surreal. Was she doing the right thing in having accepted that plug? Had she just lost a chance at all three men because she'd given in so easily and quickly? What kind of woman did they think she was, anyway?

JJ frowned and grabbed her towel. She ruffled it through her hair, taking her time drying the strands as best she could. She'd spent the past ten years in prison. She'd lost way too many years of her life sitting in a barred cage. Now she wanted to make up for lost time. She was going to do it with all three men. That they would invite themselves into her bed—JJ shivered just thinking about the idea of having all three of them making love to her at the same time.

No, she wouldn't turn down their offer. She was a woman. She had needs. She wanted to stay here for as long as she could. She liked it here. Liked them. More than liked them.

When her hair was relatively dry, she tossed the towel into the nearby hamper and then grabbed another towel.

She smiled as she began drying the rest of her. Maybe she was batshit crazy, but she did want to take this relationship with the guys to the next level? She was a grown woman and she had every right to decide whom she wanted in her bed. There was absolutely nothing wrong with that, especially if all three men were in agreement.

She wrapped her towel around her body, and knotted it at her breast. Tension and excitement zipped through her as she stepped into her bedroom. She stopped. It was semi-dark in here. Hadn't she left her bedroom light on? Her gaze snapped to her bedroom windows. To her surprise, dainty green-and-red Christmas lights blinked at the windows.

Oh how sweet. They must have done this while she'd been showering. It looked gorgeous. So Christmassy. A cozy fire crackled in her fireplace too.

They were getting her in the mood. She blew out a tense breath and she tried not to tremble at what was going to happen tonight. Movement from her bed made her cry out in surprise. She recognized Dan lying there. The covers were pulled up to his neck and he wore a cowboy hat.

Oh dear!

"Hey baby, I thought you'd never come out of that shower."

Without warning, he tossed the covers aside. In the semi-darkness, she spied powerful muscles flexing in his legs. Between his thighs, she spied a long and thick cock with a large scrotum. She swallowed as she stared. She'd had very limited experience with guys before she'd gone to prison. Just two, and they'd been awkward teenagers like her. She hadn't realized a man's erection could be so...big.

Dan patted the empty spot beside him. "Come on in and let's get you warm."

Could she really do this? Could she really go through with having sex with Dan? She trembled as she stepped forward. She wanted to. Oh, how she wanted to. It was just that reality was so different than fantasy.

"Drop the towel. I want to look at you," he instructed. His voice sounded strong, yet gentle. His gaze was lusty. Hot. He stared at her as if she were a feast.

Her cheeks warmed right along with the rest of her. Suddenly she felt like a butterfly emerging from a chrysalis. Awakening to something beautiful and free.

"Don't tell me you're shy," he whispered. A teasing grin tilted his sweet lips and her heart skipped a couple of beats. Gosh, he looked so cute when he smiled at her. He didn't wait for her to answer. Instead, he sat up and swung his legs over the edge of the bed. Then he held out his hands to her.

Emotions, thick and raw, bubbled up inside her. She was saying goodbye to their innocent relationship.

It was time. No turning back. She wanted this.

He spoke softly. "I have to tell you the truth, I'm not shy in bed. I want you. I have for some time. We all have wanted you."

She blew out a tense breath and placed her hand into his. His strong fingers curled around hers and he squeezed tenderly.

"Don't worry, I'll be gentle...at first." The last two words came out in a husky whisper that had her breath backing up in her lungs.

He pulled her toward him until she stood between his spread legs.

Don't look down, JJ. *Don't*...But even as she was thinking it, her gaze was lowering to the area between his thighs. To that magnificently large cock. It was very erect. Very swollen and...her vagina convulsed and she creamed warmly.

She licked her lips as an incredible nervous anticipation weaved around her. Dan let go of her hand and he reached up. Her skin sizzled as his finger dipped beneath the simple towel knot at her breast. He tugged and the towel dropped away. Warm air breathed against her body.

His Adam's apple bobbed and his gaze grew darker as he studied her.

"I've been dying to know how you look under all those clothes, JJ. I've been dying to touch you. To kiss you."

She yelped as he pulled her forward. She crashed down upon his length, her legs tangling with his, her naked body draping over his body. His cock pressed boldly against her tummy and his mouth seared over hers. The heat of his male skin melting against hers was surprisingly pleasing.

He let go of her hands, and then splayed them firm and hot around her waist. He pressed the thick brand of his erection tighter against her. He kissed her hard and with a desperation that made her want him even more. She curled her hands over his shoulders, her fingertips touching the hard contours of his sinewy muscles. He smelled good. Of soap and pine trees.

He tasted good too. Of the peppermint mints she loved placing on the dinner table so the men could nibble on them after supper while they played cards.

His mouth made love to her. He sipped tenderly at the edges of her lips and the confident way he kissed her chased away any lingering inner turmoil.

"I'm pretty bold. I hope I don't scare you," Dan whispered as he broke the kiss. His breathing was fast and raspy.

She didn't know what to say. Heck, she didn't think she could even talk. Her lips tickled wonderfully and her thoughts were all scattered. His huge erection continued to press boldly between her thighs.

She wanted his thick length buried inside of her.

"Are you wearing your plug?" he asked. He sucked her left earlobe into his mouth. Wicked tingles whipped through her.

She nodded.

"Good. Good."

He kissed her again. This time his mouth moved harder and fiercer over hers. Awareness shivered through her as she parted her teeth and his hot tongue dashed into her mouth. Their tongues clashed in a duel and her world tilted.

Oh!

"I want to taste you," he whispered as he suddenly broke the kiss.

Taste? Her mind was muddled. What did he mean?

In an instant, he had changed their positions. Suddenly, he was on top of her. His legs straddling her hips, his long cock branding her thighs. His eyes twinkled and he smiled as he gazed down at her.

"You're so beautiful, JJ. I don't think you realize how attractive you are."

She was?

He didn't wait for her to say thank you for his compliment or allow her to deny that she was beautiful because he dipped his head and began kissing a fiery trail across the length of her collarbone. Then he moved his body off hers, and shifted himself lower. His hot hands framed her breasts. Her heart pounded faster as his head lowered and his mouth fused over her right nipple.

Wow!

She twisted as heat enveloped her sensitive tip. She groaned as his teeth nipped gently and pleasure-pain exploded. He licked and lapped and smoothed his tongue around her areola. Her breathing quickened. Then his mouth melted over her nipple again and he suckled her. The exquisite pressure zinged sharp sensations right down to her pussy. She arched against him, needing more.

He moved his head to her other breast and his tongue worked its magic there, until she was whimpering. He dipped his head lower, kissing a fiery trail down her stomach. Her tummy quivered as his tongue seduced her skin with sultry licks and his teeth tormented her with sensual nips.

As he neared her mons, he stopped and lifted his head. His face was flushed. His eyes were dark and shone with sexual intent.

"Open your legs for me, sweetheart," he said softly.

She whimpered as she spread her thighs. She was so wet for him, and her vagina clenched as he suddenly lifted her hips and placed a pillow beneath her ass. Then he quickly maneuvered his body over her lower half. His wide shoulders pressed against the insides of her legs, preventing them from closing.

He dipped his head between her thighs and she groaned as he blew hot puffs of air against her throbbing clitoris.

"Have you ever been made love to by air?" he said and then puffed again.

Her clit was so ultra-sensitive that uncontrollable spasms zipped through her thighs and belly. She thrashed her head around on her pillow, unable to speak.

He blew against her clit again. She clenched her hands into tight knots as wicked sensations engulfed her. He was stoking a fire inside her. Something that would be uncontrollable once he ignited the fuse.

"It's been a long time since you've been with a man, hasn't it?" he asked.

She couldn't answer and he went back to blowing.

His head and shoulders were so hot between her legs. The tantalizing splash of air pummelled her clit, making her gasp and shiver. An agonizing tightness whipped through her pussy.

Oh gosh, was he going to torture her in this way?

She clenched her fists tighter as he puffed some more.

"What do you want me to do to you, baby?" he growled. She swore there was an underlying teasing in his voice. Did he know how inexperienced she was? Did he know how badly her body hurt in having to wait for him to make love to her?

"More," she gasped out the word, not really knowing how to verbalize what she wanted.

"Maybe you want this..."

He lapped at her clit with his tongue making her cry out at the exquisite pressure. Instinctively, she lifted her legs and quickly brought them up over his shoulders. She pressed the heels of her feet into his hard back muscles.

His hot mouth fused over her pussy and he sucked. She keened as an agonizing pleasure tore through her and she was instantly lost in the vortex. Her breath shuddered and her hips jerked as he licked, sipped and sucked. Every muscle inside of her tightened until tremors rocked her and she wanted to dive inside the pleasure.

Dan kept lapping, licking and sucking on her pussy. She was a feast to him, that's what she was. A banquet. Every time he sucked, her sweet cream splashed into his mouth and he eagerly drank from her. She was inexperienced. He'd been able to tell in the blush on her face and how quickly she climaxed. After he'd wrenched three orgasms out of her, he could barely stand the pulsing ache gripping his shaft. He knew he should make this last for her, but he couldn't control himself anymore. He needed to have her. Now!

He moved his head away from her steaming pussy and then he quickly climbed over her.

Her eyes suddenly blinked open and his heart melted at the satisfaction and glittering lust in her gaze. She had enjoyed what he'd done to her. She would enjoy many more nights at his hands and those of Brady and Rafe. She would know she was needed and loved.

"One more important thing," he whispered.

She whimpered in response and he reached over to grab one of the condoms he'd placed near one of the pillows when he'd first climbed into her bed.

With his teeth, he tore away the top of the package. A moment later, he sheathed his aching shaft. Bringing her to satisfaction had just about killed him. His cock was near to bursting and his balls hurt like hell from wanting her.

There was no more time for foreplay. The time for action was now.

He moaned as he positioned himself on top of her, his shaft spearing quickly into her in one harsh thrust. She gasped and bucked beneath him. Her hands slapped over his shoulders and her nails dug painfully into his muscles.

Her pussy clenched tightly around his cock and intense pleasure grabbed him. He withdrew and thrust his swollen shaft into her again. She writhed beneath him. Her wiggles created more friction and pleasure. His vision darkened and he lost it.

He began pistoning into her pussy. His thrusts were deep and uncontrolled. Beneath him, she gasped and moaned. Her fingers dug harder into his back. Her eyes were scrunched and her lips parted slightly. She wailed as she came. The erotic sounds were music to his ears.

He closed his eyes. He kissed her and drowned himself within her exhilarating heat. He thrust harder and faster and her vaginal muscles clenched sweetly around his shaft like a vise. Suddenly, he was rumbling within the ecstasy, drowning inside the exquisite convulsions. He was lost within her.

There was no way they were going back to what they had before. He'd branded her, and she belonged to him now.

Brady grit his teeth as his shaft jerked against the tight restraint of his jeans. JJ's sweet little cries were drifting all the way down the stairs and into the living room where he and Rafe had remained, playing a game of solitaire after Dan had gone upstairs to be with JJ.

"Man, this is killing me," Rafe grumbled as he stared at the stairwell.

"You, me and my cock. But we all agreed to stick with the plan and break her in gently," Brady replied.

"Doesn't sound like Dan's breaking her in gently." Rafe retorted. He swore beneath his breath as another erotic cry swept through the room.

Brady closed his eyes and counted to five. He needed to steady his breathing. Needed to get out of the house and into the cold air so he could think.

"I'm going out," he said between gritted teeth. If he stuck around and listened to any more, he would lose it, go up those stairs four at a time and take JJ himself.

"Better check on the new calves. Maybe throw down some more hay for their bedding. It's going to be a cold night," Rafe said thickly.

Yeah, and a cold shower for Brady.

"Whose fucking stupid idea was this to take her one at a time?" Brady grumbled as he stood. He winced at the tightness between his thighs.

"Yours," Rafe hissed in a not-so-friendly tone.

"Next time I come up with a stupid idea like that, shoot me, will you?"

"It'll be my pleasure."

Another sultry moan from JJ echoed down the stairs and through the room.

"I'm going out to check on the cattle in the north pasture," Rafe said as he stood and followed Brady into the mudroom. They began donning their winter gear.

Surprise made Brady frown. "Now? You know it's dangerous to ride out after dark," Brady warned.

"It's a hell of a lot more dangerous staying in here listening to her. I need to get out of here or our plan is going to crumble. Comprendez?"

Brady nodded and slipped on his wool hat.

"Understood." And he wasn't kidding. The last thing he wanted to do was scare JJ right out of their lives. If she discovered all three of them wanted to fuck her, she'd probably dial her parole officer herself and ask to be flown back to prison. Having her out of his life was the last thing he wanted. They would take it slow. They had to.

He couldn't get out the door fast enough.

JJ awoke on a moan. She'd slept so deeply and so soundly that when she blinked her eyes open, she didn't even know where she was or why her pussy, lips and nipples were so...pleasantly sore.

And in one wild wave it all came tumbling back. She'd slept with Dan! Was he still in bed beside her? Had he stayed all night? Early morning sunshine sparkled through the bedroom window panes illuminating her cozy room. Her tummy dropped. She'd always gotten up at the crack of dawn to prepare breakfast for the guys. It was late.

Yet she didn't want to move. She'd never felt so comfortable. Never had wanted so badly to just lie in bed and enjoy the memories of what had happened last night.

Dan had been perfect. He'd wrenched orgasms out of her so easily that she doubted she would ever go back to masturbating. She silenced her breathing and listened. No sounds. Not even a breath from Dan. Tentatively, she reached out behind her. Her hand landed on cold emptiness.

A frisson of disappointment made her frown. Dan was gone. How long had he stayed? The last thing she remembered was him spooning his naked body against her backside. Had she not been exhausted from all those cries and shudders and tossing around, she would have told him to slide his cock into her vagina so she could sleep with his shaft buried inside of her.

JJ closed her eyes and blew out a tense breath. Just thinking about what had happened last night was tensing her up again. The only thing she wanted to do right now was to have sex. She opened her eyes and stared at the fireplace. A couple of split birch logs crackled as flames licked around them. The sounds were loud. Her cries while she'd come last night had been a heck of a lot louder.

Heat fused into her cheeks. No doubt that Brady and Rafe had heard. How could they not? How could she face them? Maybe she didn't have to. The house was too quiet. They must have made their own breakfasts and left for the day. Running a ranch was a full-time job, and she needed to get her ass out of bed.

Reluctantly, JJ whipped aside her covers and rolled out of bed. As she grabbed the towel she'd dropped on the floor last night, she spied something light brown hanging on the post by the foot of her bed. She grinned. She had her first cowboy hat on her bed post.

Suddenly she couldn't wait until all three cowboys hats were there.

After a quick shower, JJ slipped into a pair of jeans and a red blouse. When she opened her bedroom door and stepped into the hallway, the aromatic scent of coffee had her hurrying down the stairs.

Coffee. That's exactly what she needed. When she reached the bottom of the stairs, she skidded to a halt. The table had been set for her. A couple of candles flickered in candle holders and a red poinsettia plant had been set there as well.

Where in the world had that plant come from? How had they been able to keep it hidden from her? She laughed as she strolled to the table and picked up the plant. Tears bubbled into her eyes. She hadn't seen a real poinsettia plant since she was a kid.

This plant was the most beautiful thing she had ever seen. She stared at it for the longest time, admiring the red and green leaves, committing it to memory. Finally, the scent of coffee urged her to place the plant back onto the table. A couple of minutes later, she was sitting in front of the poinsettia plant, a cup of steaming coffee in hand and with a note she'd found by the machine.

The note was from Dan.

JJ,

Blizzard coming. Driving the pregnant cows in. We won't be back until supper. Enjoy your breakfast. Last night was great. Rafe will be with you tonight.

Dan

JJ worried her bottom lip as she read the last line. Last night was great. Had Rafe and Brady seen the note?

She slapped the paper onto the table, rolled her eyes and laughed. Even if they hadn't read it, they would have heard her last night.

Heat flushed her cheeks. How embarrassing. Why couldn't she just act casually about what had happened? Why did she feel shy about sex? She'd enjoyed it so much. Yet, she just couldn't get comfortable with the idea of facing Brady and Rafe, or even Dan, tonight.

Goodness, even her hands were shaking. She held them out in front of her and sure enough, they were trembling. Her pussy was clenching too as she thought about Dan's big body coming over her, his thick, hard shaft penetrating her and his mouth claiming hers.

Oh dear. It was going to be a very long day.

"Heard you come in really late last night," Dan said as the three of them tied off their horses on a couple of saplings in the north meadow. There was a teasing tone to Dan's voice and Rafe wasn't in the mood for his taunting today. They'd worked hard to separate the pregnant cattle from the rest of the wild herd and then led them into the corrals near the barn so they could keep an eye on them during the blizzard.

"Your turn to listen tonight," Rafe grumbled. He'd been dying since hearing JJ's sexy little mews, and he couldn't wait to see her when they got back to the ranch house.

"Let's not talk about our nights. We agreed to stick to business talks during the days." Brady replied curtly.

He looked as grumpy as Rafe felt as he dragged out their lunch from his saddlebags and trudged to a nearby fallen log. He kicked off a good amount of snow so they could all sit.

Dan grabbed a couple of Thermos of coffee out of his saddlebag and winked at Rafe.

"She's well worth the wait."

"Good to know. Now shut up. I'm hungry," Rafe said. He didn't meant to be curt with Dan but he always got in a sour mood when he was tired. He knew this one-on-one sex with JJ was a temporary thing, but his cock was aching and he just wanted to be with her. Knowing that she was wearing a butt plug didn't help any either. He was an butt man and he couldn't wait to take her tight, sweet ass.

"How many more cows do we need to round up?" Brady asked as they sat down on the log on either side of him.

"Twenty-one. Then the afternoon chores need doing," Dan said. "I'll do Rafe's for him, since he came in so late last night. I'm assuming that's my fault."

There was that teasing tone in Dan's voice again. Rafe stifled his irritation. "I'd appreciate it," he said. He accepted a Thermos from Dan, unscrewed the lid and poured some coffee into his tin cup. The warm steam from the coffee felt good as it wafted against his cold cheeks. Doing his chores was the least Dan could do after chasing him out of the warm house into the frigid weather last night.

They ate in silence amidst white puffs of steam uncurling from their cups and their noses. The air was colder than usual, despite the clear blue skies. The blizzard was still a couple of days away, but they would need all that time to get the at-risk cows settled, some more firewood dragged in and piled against the mudroom walls and near the several fireplaces in the house. Plus the generators had to be checked and ready to go at a moment's notice. This would be on top of their regular chores of getting feed out to the wild cattle and checking fence lines and other things.

Rafe smiled as he chewed on the delicious roast beef sandwich Brady had whipped up for them. It was going to be a Christmas Eve and Christmas Day blizzard. He always liked it when it snowed on Christmas. Up until his late teens, he'd never seen snow. He'd lived in southern Florida and it rarely got below freezing in the area where he'd lived with his parents and siblings.

The minute he'd graduated high school he'd left home, wanting to travel the world. He didn't get far on the money he'd saved from his after school and summer jobs, so he'd gotten a job working on the shipping docks in Boston. Then, when he'd gotten bored, he'd done gigs on lobster and fishing boats in the Maritimes and New England states.

Over the past twelve years, he'd worked in several states as well as a few provinces and couple of territories in Canada. He'd plowed farmers' fields in the Saskatchewan prairies, heli-logged in the British Columbia interior and then cattle ranched in Wyoming and Montana.

He'd been in Toronto, visiting his sister who'd moved there with her Canadian husband, when he'd gone to a downtown bar for a drink and had overheard Brady and Dan chatting about plans to create a cattle ranch up in Northern Ontario. Brady had been bored with his lawyer job and Dan had been going nuts as a chiropractor.

The idea of cattle ranching in the secluded Northern Ontario wilderness had struck him as adventurous so he'd introduced himself and offered his manual labor services. He'd been having a great time since then. But then JJ had come along, and he'd begun to feel as if something had been missing in his life. He'd finally realized he needed JJ to fill his ache. Dan and Brady had realized the same thing.

When Brady had mentioned he was falling for her, and Dan had expressed the same feelings, Rafe had quickly come to the conclusion that he didn't want to leave this place. Nor did he want to lose his friendship with Rafe or Dan—or with JJ, for that matter. The idea of sharing her had been met with enthusiasm by all three of them.

She just fit. All four of them fit. He wouldn't dream of ruining it. He would stick with the plan. One-on-one sexual relationships until she was comfortable, and then they would up it to ménages. He inhaled a deep breath of the cold air and accepted a second roast beef sandwich from Brady.

Was he being a selfish asshole in wanting to share her? Didn't she deserve the traditional one guy who would put her on a pedestal and worship her?

He shook his head. No, she deserved *three* guys who would do that.

Chapter Eight

JJ blew out a tense breath as she stepped into the shower. It had been a very long day, especially with anticipating sex tonight as well as waiting to face the three guys again. Thankfully, they'd been gentlemen tonight. She'd expected some sort of kidding regarding her cries of pleasure last night, but they'd barely deviated from their routine of discussing what needed to be done regarding the ranch.

But their heated looks when they watched her approach the table with their food, or their lingering gazes when they thought she wasn't looking as she'd cooked, brought intense awareness about them. She'd found herself gazing into the shiny stainless-steel pots and catching them studying her.

Wild excitement roared through her every time she thought about one of them coming up behind her, and undressing her right there in front of the other two. But it hadn't happened.

Whew! *Have mercy*! She was getting too hot thinking about it. She needed to grab a shower and not think about Rafe joining her in bed tonight. But she couldn't stop fantasizing as she undressed and then leaned in and turned on the shower.

What kind of lover would Rafe be? When she'd shared that kiss with him, sitting on his lap, she'd instinctively known he would be attentive. Would he be as intense and bold like Dan? She sensed he would be.

All three men were strong. They had to be to live in this solitude, driving their cattle from meadow to meadow when the snow melted. They'd carved a cattle ranch out of the wilderness. They'd done long cattle drives through forests and across rivers to a railroad many miles away where the animals were loaded into railcars. The guys were always working outdoors coming in only to eat and now...to have sex with her.

JJ smiled as she stepped under the steamy spray of the shower. She could think of worse things a woman would have to endure.

Christmas with her cowboys. Cowboys for Christmas. Two more days until the Christmas Day. She had a perfect holiday dinner planned for them. There were several frozen turkeys and hams in the freezers. She would make one of each. It would allow her to use the turkey and ham for sandwiches for several days afterward, too. She'd freeze the bones and make soup from them in January when the real cold hit.

She couldn't wait to make stuffing for the turkey. She'd seen canned cranberries in the basement pantry and she'd make mashed potatoes from the potato supply Dan had harvested from his garden and stashed in the cellar. She'd also made her first order for food supplies over the Internet, and ordered some Christmas presents for the guys with the money they'd deposited in an online bank account they'd set up for her.

North Country Air had emailed her back and said they would confirm a delivery date. She doubted they would come before Christmas with the blizzard warning, but that was okay. All she wanted for Christmas this year were her sexy cowboys.

She laughed as she angled her face beneath the spray. Who knew she would turn out to be the domestic type? But she loved it. She loved cooking for them. She treasured them. How could it be possible that she had such affection for three men in such a short time? Her heart melted whenever she looked at each one of them.

The guys had said they could be snowed in here until May. If they were lucky, the weather would warm up by then and Dan could start his garden in June. But what in the world would they do until then? To her amazement, thinking about being trapped here with her three men and with no way out didn't bring the familiar claustrophobia.

It brought her happiness. If they were snowed in, she couldn't be returned to prison if she did something wrong, right? And best of all, they would love her and make love to her. Gosh, what had she done right in her life to deserve such happiness? She'd endured her stepfather's beatings and his abuse of her mother just to get to this point. It was almost worth the ten years behind bars to get to this point.

A movement from the corner of her eye caught her attention. As she turned, she spied Rafe stepping into the shower. Wicked shudders of anticipation scampered through her and raced directly into her pussy, making it clench. The need for penetration was so intense she couldn't stop the whimper from escaping her mouth.

As he slid the shower door closed, muscles rippled all over him. His shoulders, his chest and his abdomen. There wasn't an ounce of fat on the guy. He was lean and fit from hard physical work.

Her breath caught as she dropped her gaze to between his thighs. His cock was fully erect and sheathed in a clear condom. His flesh was shaded an angry purple and his shaft was ultra-thick and about eight inches long.

Oh dear. Oh my.

When he reached down and stroked his swollen length, she watched in wonder as his shaft jerked.

"I've been waiting too long to take you, JJ. Too long," he said.

She forced herself to lift her gaze and caught his heated look. He smiled and her heart skipped a beat. Any shyness at him seeing her naked totally vanished.

"I couldn't wait until you got out of the shower," he confessed.

"I guess I'm going to have to expect these unexpected visits."

Goodness, her legs felt weak and trembly at the intense way he studied at her. His eyes were darkening as he stepped toward her.

Her pulse pounded with anticipation. Heated blood flowed through her veins.

He stopped a couple of inches away. His body heat wrapped around her and she could smell an erotic spicy scent wafting off him. She really liked it.

"You smell nice," she whispered.

"You do too.". He inhaled deeply and closed his eyes. He seemed to drift away for a moment, but then his eyes popped open again. His gaze was intense as he stared at her with a fierceness she'd not seen in him before.

"Baby, I don't know how long I can hold out. Listening to you and Dan last night..." His words trailed away.

He *had* heard her cries. She blew out a tense breath.

"I just want to make you cry out like that again. It was the sweetest sound."

Oh my.

Without warning, he reached out and cupped her breasts. His palms were hot against her flesh and awareness skipped through her as he dipped his head and sucked her left nipple into his mouth.

Using his face, he pushed against her breast, bringing her gently beneath the shower spray. The warm liquid pounded over her head, and she blinked the water out of her eyes.

He continued to press against her until her back was up against the wall. The tiles were cold against her backside and the shower spray danced off his left shoulder.

They were belly to belly and she gasped as he pressed his cock head against her clit. He teased and pushed against her bundle of nerves until pleasure consumed her.

The rasp of stubble against her breast and the pressure of his lips as he suckled her nipple sent shivers racing through her. She slipped her hands over his big shoulders and enjoyed the hard feel of his muscles beneath her fingers.

He moved his mouth to her other breast. His tongue flicked against her bud. It beaded. He stroked her until she was aching. Then he sucked her nipple into his mouth. The heat was exquisite. He nipped at her tender flesh and shivers thrashed through her.

She moaned softly. He growled in response. Her knees weakened at the sultry sound. Her hands tangled into his wet hair.

Shock rushed through her as he grabbed her by her wrists and stretched her arms over her head, holding her wrists captive against the wall, quickly putting her into a submissive position. He inched his cock into her pussy. Her vaginal muscles clenched tightly around the thick intrusion. He was big. Thicker than she'd anticipated.

Panic skittered through her. No one had held her captive like this. Ever.

"I can see fear in your eyes. Don't be afraid of me. Sometimes I can be rough, but never be afraid. I know what I'm doing," Rafe whispered huskily.

"I'm not." But she was. Kind of. Maybe. The heated way he was looking at her made an unpredictable desire roar through her. She had no control over his power. No control over him. She kind of liked it.

"I can be intense. Just know I will never hurt you intentionally. Trust me."

She believed him. But still, being in this stimulating position of vulnerability was a foreign feeling.

"I want to make love to you so bad." His eyes glazed and his dark lashes lowered.

She closed her eyes and melted beneath him as his firm mouth swept over hers in a demanding kiss that sucked away all thoughts of protest.

She creamed beneath the assault of his kiss. He moved harder against her and pressed his heavy cock deeper into her. The pressure of his shaft sinking into her was incredible. His girth pushed past protesting muscles and she inhaled into his mouth at the sweet bite of pain.

He withdrew quickly, then slid in again. This time deeper. She could feel his pulsing veins pressing against her protesting vaginal muscles and moaned at the bursts of pleasure-pain. He withdrew again, then poised his cock head at her entrance.

She moaned in disappointment. She wanted him thrusting into her. Wanted to buck and cry out as he made her climax.

His lips sipped at hers tenderly and his free hand managed to dip between their bodies. He touched her clit and teasingly caressed. She shuddered and just about came on the spot.

He kissed her harder, rubbing her until carnal sensations curled around her. Her breathing quickened. Her body tightened.

His wicked tongue speared past her lips and into her mouth. The intrusion rocked her. He was moving so fast, it made her heady. She struggled to keep up with his kisses, but he overpowered her in a very intoxicating way.

She keened as he rocked his hips and drove his solid flesh into her again. Fireworks exploded behind her eyes. She ripped her mouth from his and cried out and then gasped for air as she convulsed. His hand left her and a moment later his fingers slipped beneath her chin.

He held her firmly, his mouth slanting over hers again. He consumed her with a heat-seeking kiss that shattered her mind and weakened her legs.

She bucked against him. Struggled against him as pleasure drowned her. Her pussy greedily sucked at his shaft. With his every stroke, her vagina clutched desperately at his thickness. She struggled to free her wrists from his grasp, but he held her tight and continued powering into her with wicked, solid strokes, making her cry out over and over again as she came.

Rafe was out of control. He knew he was on a sharp edge after finding her naked in the shower. Seeing that vulnerable look glazing her eyes as he captured her wrists and held her captive had turned him on big time. Touching her velvety breasts, taking her nipples into her mouth, heaven.

He'd wanted to go slow with her. Tame her with his gentleness. But he was tired of waiting for her. He was desperate. Needy. He craved to be inside her. Wanted to make her belong to him.

He was losing it and he was helpless to stop himself. Her pussy was deliciously tight as he feverishly thrust into her velvety depths. He could smell her cream wafting up with the steam from the shower. He relished capturing her cries and gasps in his mouth and enjoyed how her sweet lips submitted to his force. The feel of her body bucking and gyrating against his drove him wild.

Man! She was perfection! He fucked her with hard, heavy strokes.

Her struggles and her spasming pussy aroused him as no other woman had. Breathtaking sensations curled up and down his shaft. Sharp blades of pleasure spiraled out of nowhere and engulfed him. His cock jerked inside her and he came. Hard.

Convulsions captured him. They were piercing and taut and they dragged him under and into a pleasure-soaked, chaotic world he just didn't want to climb out of.

He was lost inside her.

If Rafe hadn't been leaning against her, his cock still impaling her, she might have slipped right down onto the shower stall floor. The man had literally rocked her world. She stood, her back against the wall, her arms being held captive by his one hand. Her heart pounded frantically against her chest and her pussy continued to spasm around his spent shaft.

Mercy! But he knew how to fuck. She felt dazed, disoriented and very satisfied.

"Someone's at the door," Rafe murmured.

She thought he was kidding, so she just enjoyed the after-sex haze sifting through her and melted against him, enjoying the powerful muscles flex against her belly.

But then he moaned and brought her arms down and let go of her wrists.

What? Was he serious? She'd been hoping for another round. Or two. Or maybe even three?

She blinked open her eyes in time to see him frowning and shaking his head. He turned off the water and JJ gasped at the noise of someone frantically knocking on the door.

How in the world hadn't she heard that?

"This'd better be good!" he shouted angrily.

"Just got a call from Kelly." It was Brady. "She needs to land her plane on the lake. She's got an emergency. We need everyone down there. Dan I and I will prepare a landing for her."

A sense of urgency whipped through JJ at the concern lacing Brady's voice.

Rafe gazed at her and shook his head. His eyes flashed with disappointment. "Sorry baby, we need to help out."

JJ nodded. "Of course."

He withdrew his cock from her pussy and a moment later they both stepped out of the shower stall.

"We'll be down in a minute. We'll get the lanterns started," Rafe called out.

"Kelly needs first-aid services too. She's got Blue on board and she's gone into labor. She's ready to give birth, like, *yesterday*."

"I'll get the kit." Rafe called.

When no answer came, JJ assumed Brady had left.

Rafe swore softly beneath his breath. "Blue's gone into labor early."

JJ tossed him a towel and he began drying himself.

"Blue?" This was the first time she'd heard mention of this person.

"She's a bush pilot with North Country Air. She's not due for at least another month."

"Oh. So you know first aid? I thought Dan was the one who did the short stint in pharmaceutical school?"

"We've both taken courses."

He dried himself in record time. Then he slid on his underwear, followed by his jeans.

"Have you ever delivered a baby?" she asked as hurriedly dried herself.

Rafe grinned and shrugged. "No, but I've delivered calves. How hard can delivering a human baby be? Make sure your hair is dry or you'll catch pneumonia. Meet you downstairs in about fifteen?"

JJ nodded.

"Oh, and baby, you were awesome. We'll have to do it again, really soon." Rafe winked. He zipped up his jeans and slipped out the door.

JJ smiled, quickly grabbed the blow dryer and began drying her hair. She loved his confidence. He knew how to fuck her into a quick and quite satisfying orgasm and it seemed he wasn't afraid of delivering a baby, despite his inexperience. Her liking for Rafe just flew up a bunch of notches. Once again, she was struck with wondering what she'd done right in her life to deserve being here surrounded by three magnificent cowboys.

"Push, Blue! Push now!" Rafe shouted at the thirtysomething blonde-haired woman named Blue, who was frantically panting while scrunched in a seated position on the backseat of the same small plane that JJ had arrived here over a month ago. The lower half of Blue's body was partially hidden by a blanket draped over her knees. Rafe sat on a wine crate hunched in front of Blue while JJ stood behind him and held up a storm lantern so he could see what he was doing.

"I'm pushing!" the woman shouted. Anger flared in her dark-blue eyes and perspiration glistened on her forehead. She clenched her fists, closed her eyes and began to push again. Her face turned red in the light.

Everything had happed so quickly after Brady had knocked on the bathroom door. She'd met Rafe in the mudroom, where they'd dressed in their winter gear. Rafe had slung a large knapsack full of first-aid supplies onto his back and grabbed JJ's hand, leading her outdoors into the darkness.

Icy-cold air had sucked the breath right out of her lungs as they'd stomped along a plowed trail that led down to the lake. On the ice, Dan and Brady were driving large snowblowers and plowing snow to form a large landing path on the lake. Rafe and JJ had quickly grabbed lanterns out of a shed near the shoreline, lit them and to set the lamps along the edges of the plowed area. Kelly had arrived several minutes later, her plane roaring over the treetops and setting down as smooth as silk on the cleared area on the ice.

It was the first time in JJ's life that she actually wished to be brave like Kelly and fly a small airplane. But then the familiar terror had clawed somewhere deep in the back of her mind and she'd cancelled that thought, pushing it back down where it had come from so she could concentrate on helping Rafe.

"The baby is here. The head is out. One more push, Blue. Make it a big one." Rafe's voice was calmer now. Almost soothing. Emotions clutched at JJ as Blue smiled, scrunched her eyes closed and gave another push.

A few minutes later, JJ held a cleaned-up screaming baby girl wrapped snugly in a thick fleece blanket, while Rafe assisted Blue onto the back of a snowmobile that Brady had brought earlier along with water and clean towels.

"She's beautiful, isn't she?" Brady said as he stood beside JJ and peered at the infant.

JJ wished she could speak, but she swore if she did, she would cry. The infant was the sweetest-looking thing she'd ever seen in her life. Just looking at her made her both happy and weepy at the same time.

"Please, I want to hold my baby," Blue whispered as she held out her hands from the back of the snowmobile.

JJ carefully handed Blue her newborn. The woman smiled and cuddled the baby to her chest. A moment later, the snowmobile roared to life and Rafe drove toward the ranch, leaving JJ and Brady alone.

"Are you okay? You're kind of quiet." Brady asked. The sweet, concerned look on his face melted away her weepy emotions. Happiness whipped through her.

"I just witnessed a miracle, Brady. A miracle."

His smile widened. "That you did. Why don't you head up to the ranch and I'll douse the lanterns and bring up the supplies that Kelly brought."

"Kelly brought the supplies?"

"Yeah, she said she sent an email that she was delivering the stuff you ordered and she was coming tonight. You didn't get it?"

She shook her head. "No, I didn't even check the emails. I figured they wouldn't come until after Christmas."

"Actually North Country flies pretty much from sunup to sundown seven days a week. The woman who runs the business is a real workaholic. I guess I should have warned you that when you place an order with them, you can pretty much expect it anytime."

"I'll remember that. But I need for you to do me one favor."

"What's that?"

"Don't open anything. I'd like to do that. Okay?"

He looked at her kind of funny and she hoped he didn't suspect anything. Her presents for the guys would be packed in with the food supplies.

"It's my job and I love doing stuff like that. Will you promise?"

He smiled and her tummy did an awesome flip that she really liked.

"I promise, JJ girl."

Oh, he'd just given her a nickname. She liked it.

He handed her a lantern and nodded toward the ranch house. "Okay, so hurry on up. I want you out of this cold before you catch one."

She turned, and before she could walk away, he gave her a hot swat right on her ass.

She yelped and spun back around, almost dropping the lantern. His heated gaze made more of those excited flips tremble through her belly.

"Expect more of those tomorrow tonight."

She nodded jerkily. He liked to spank? She'd never been spanked by a guy before. She could hardly wait to experience it.

She couldn't get up to the ranch house fast enough. She wanted to hold that cute baby in her arms again, and then she needed to get the butt plug switched to the biggest size.

Chapter Nine

"Wow, you're up early." Kelly's hushed voice made JJ look up from the third cup of steaming coffee she'd been nursing. It was five o'clock and Kelly looked angelic. Her cheeks were flushed pink, her blonde hair was a tousled mess and she was wrapped in Brady's dark-brown fleece robe. Not an ounce of makeup on her face and the woman could pose as a model, she was so pretty.

Seeing Kelly wrapped in Brady's robe shot a sharp bite of jealousy through JJ, but she clamped down on it. Brady had been kind enough to give up his bed to Kelly, Blue and her newborn. He'd moved to the guest bedroom upstairs. Yet it made JJ uneasy seeing this gorgeous, confident woman in the ranch house

"I didn't go to bed," JJ admitted.

"Insomnia? I've had my share." Kelly moved to the coffeepot and poured herself a cup.

Oh, lady, if you only knew what was keeping me up. Her pussy throbbed with the need of having a swollen, hard cock thrusting into her again. Her nipples ached from Rafe's mouth nibbling on them. Heck, they'd still been pleasantly sore from Dan's tender suckling. And she was supposed to sleep with Brady tonight? She creamed warmly at discovering a note from him on her bed when she'd gone in to change earlier. In the note, he'd said he was looking forward to being with her tonight.

Mercy, she wasn't sure how she was going to make it through today, when all she could think about was having sex with Brady. Her body longed for his touches, and she ached to have him kiss her like he'd done that first night. She blew out a tense breath and tried to steady her breathing.

A moment later, Kelly sat down beside JJ at the dining table. She gazed at the nearby Christmas tree where the dainty white lights twinkled and then at the frosted windows where more lights sparkled.

"Wow, you really decked this place out. When I was here last Christmas dropping some stuff off, the guys hadn't done a thing for the holidays."

"They're busy. They work so hard they barely have time to eat, but they did take me out to get a tree and then they helped me decorate it."

"I'm impressed. Your living room looks stunning. It should be in a magazine."

Pride whipped through JJ as Kelly smiled warmly and they both sipped her coffee in silence for a couple of awkward minutes.

"So? How is it going since I last saw you?" Kelly asked.

JJ looked up to see Kelly staring at her with sharp blue eyes. Did she know that JJ was having sex with Rafe and Dan? Had the guys told her something?

She shrugged and averted her gaze. To her horror, her cheeks began to flame.

"Hmm, interesting reaction. So, I take it everything is going along wonderfully?"

JJ nodded.

To her surprise, Kelly placed a hand over JJ's wrist and squeezed gently.

"They are sweet men. You'll do really good if you catch one of them."

One of them. Lordy, what would Kelly say if JJ told her she'd caught *all* of them? That *all* of them wanted to have sex with her?

Her cheeks grew even hotter.

"How are your panic attacks going?" Kelly asked.

JJ tensed. How did she know about her medical condition?

"You told me about your problem when you were drunk," Kelly replied, obviously reading JJ's surprise.

"Oh." Now that Kelly mentioned it, she did kind of remember saying something to Kelly about being afraid of enclosed areas.

"I've had one big attack and have managed to keep others at bay. But they're nothing compared to the ones I had in prison."

"Well, being caged up would certainly freak me out. I don't know how you could last all those years. I would go nuts. You're so strong."

JJ laughed. Was Kelly for real? "I'm anything but strong."

Kellie looked stunned. She shook her head and disbelief edged her expression. "Don't underestimate yourself, JJ. Most city women would snap out here within a week."

JJ blinked. *They would*?

"You're a tough woman. A pioneer. I knew you were perfect for this place the minute I saw you. You are perfect for these guys. You'll last, and I am sure one of the boys will end up marrying you. If not all of them."

Oh dear. If you only knew what was going on.

Kelly laughed and winked. She took a sip of the coffee and grimaced as she swallowed.

"Now this is what I call coffee. Perfect," Kelly said.

"She is, isn't she." Brady's voice echoed as he stepped off the bottom step and strolled into the kitchen. He wore nothing but a pair of jeans. Muscles rippled across his back and biceps as he poured himself a cup of coffee.

"Wow! He's hot!" Kelly mouthed the words at JJ and winked.

JJ frowned as irritation snapped through her. This was the first time she'd seen Brady without his shirt on. He'd never done this before. At least not in front of her.

Bastard. Was he showing off his hunky body to Kelly, trying to impress her?

Brady came to stand in front of them. He smiled first at Kelly, then at JJ.

"JJ is perfect for this place and for us. We couldn't have asked for anyone better. I doubt there is anyone better out there for us."

"My, you speak highly of her. If I didn't know any better, I'd say there was something going on between the two of you." Kelly said as she stared up at Brady. She arched a perfectly groomed eyebrow in question at him.

Brady didn't so much as flinch. Yet she thought she saw a flare of interest in his eyes.

"Sorry, ladies. I'd like to stay and chat and give away all my secrets, but I need to get to my office and check my email for an important message. Continue on with your conversation."

JJ blew out a soft breath as she watched him stroll down the hallway. The seductive way his jeans hugged his ass made her want to cup his cheeks in her hands or, better yet, to grab his hand and drag him off to her bed.

"I'm sorry, I was just teasing him," Kelly giggled as she focused her attention back to JJ.

Just teasing? Her hopes deflated. She'd thought that Kelly had been serious. For a minute there, she'd felt as if there really could be something between her and the guys. Maybe they just wanted sex and that was it? Maybe she was being naive in wanting more?

"What's wrong? You look as if you suddenly lost your best friend. Was it something I said?"

JJ shook her head. "Just realized it's getting late and I need to get started on preparing breakfast."

Kelly looked horrified. "Now? It's like what?" She glanced at her watch. "It's not even five-thirty and you haven't even slept."

"That's ranch life. You have to get up earlier than the fish if you want to survive out here. I'll just pop into a quick shower. Breakfast is within the hour."

JJ ignored Kelly's frown as she quickly left the table. Kelly was right, though. She suddenly did feel as if she'd lost a best friend. Maybe three of them.

It had turned into a hectic day, especially with a cute newborn garnering everyone's attention and distracting the men from their chores. Now as she stared at Kelly's bright-red Cessna as it roared into the sky and disappeared over the treetops with Kelly, Blue and her baby, who Blue had named Ivy, all JJ wanted to do was crawl into bed and sleep forever.

Maybe that was why she was feeling so weepy and sad. Maybe it had nothing to do with that innocent comment from Kelly this morning about her teasing Brady about there being something between them. There was *something* between Dan, Rafe, Brady and herself. Whatever it was, she was going to enjoy it.

"You were asking Kelly a lot of questions about her plane today. I thought planes scared you?" Brady said as the two of them turned and trudged up the trail toward the ranch house. It was midafternoon and the sky was such a bright blue with the snow sparkling a gorgeous white, that it was hard to believe that by this time tomorrow they would be in the throes of a blizzard.

"I've come to a realization that I am not afraid of anything."

Brady chuckled. "You're not, eh? Not even of the big bad wolf?"

JJ frowned. He wasn't being serious. But she wouldn't expect him to be. He was a confident man and he would have no idea of what she was experiencing when she had an attack. She'd thought they came out of the blue, but Kelly had told her it could have to do with her own thoughts. Could her own thoughts be scaring her?

"Kelly suggested there was nothing to be afraid of but fear itself. She said she's going to send me some self-help books for my anxiety, panic and claustrophobia problems. She said maybe my cognitive thinking needs to change to something more positive. Instead of thinking that I can't do something, I have to train my brain into thinking I can."

"You're a strong woman, JJ. I'm sure you can get an upper hand on it."

Wow. He thought she was strong and Kelly had said the same thing early this morning. Maybe she'd been shortchanging herself? Maybe she was tougher than she'd thought?

When they entered the mudroom, JJ began to remove her scarf, but Brady suddenly grabbed her wrist. Surprise made her blink up at him. There was something intoxicating in the way he was suddenly looking at her, and an unexpected wave of heat whipped through her body.

"Hold on a minute. There's something I need to tell you, JJ girl," he whispered.

Instead of letting go of her, he suddenly pulled her against him. In a wink of an eye, she was pressed up against a wall of muscle. Before she could even comprehend what was happening, Brady's face lowered to hers and his sweet warm lips melted over hers.

Heat rolled through her. He was branding her. Teaching her how to kiss as his mouth demanded and coaxed her to open to him. He slid his tongue inside and stroked against hers until she shivered beneath the onslaught of excitement.

Hunger rose inside her and she moved against his body. Pushing her breasts against his chest, pressing her pussy against the erection tenting his jeans.

When she heard Dan and Rafe talking in the dining room, he abruptly stopped kissing her. He moved his mouth against her ear and caressed her cheek, his bristles creating sparks of feeling against her sensitive skin.

"It's not the same between all of us anymore, is it?" he said in a low voice.

She shook her head. "It's...more intense," she admitted.

"After tonight, expect more intensity. Anticipate more spontaneity. After tonight, the three of us will be taking you whenever we want. Whenever you want."

She tensed at his words. Creamed into her panties. Her mouth grew dry with a sudden nervousness.

He pulled away, letting go of her hands. She opened her eyes to find a sweet smile tilting his lips.

"See you tonight," Brady whispered.

He opened the door and stomped out of the mudroom, back outside. She barely felt the icy tendrils of air whisper against her too-warm face as she watched him saunter along the snowy trail toward the barn.

Yeah, see you.

Have mercy! Her legs were trembling from that kiss and from what he'd just said. She was surprised she was still standing.

JJ reached out and grabbed the back of one of the several chairs that lined the wall of the mudroom. She needed to steady herself. Big time. If he was this potent during daylight, then she could only imagine how intense he would be tonight.

Suddenly getting some sleep was the last thing on her mind.

"Dinner was absolutely fantastic, JJ. As always," Rafe grinned as he leaned back in his chair and patted his stomach.

"You know what they say, the fastest way to a man's heart is through his belly," Dan chuckled as he joined Rafe in leaning back in his chair and patting his stomach as well.

"You boys will have me blushing in no time flat with all your lovely compliments," JJ said with a laugh as she strolled to the fridge for dessert.

They were so sweet with their comments and momentary happiness flowed through her. But it didn't last. Brady hadn't returned for dinner and despite Rafe and Dan reassuring her that he was fine, she was worried. He never missed a meal. Except for a couple of times, and it had been expected.

"What's for dessert?" Dan called out as she opened the fridge.

She didn't answer them as she lifted the trifle dish, keeping her body between the dessert and the men's curious gazes she placed the dish onto the counter. Then, from the fridge, she grabbed another dish with the crushed items she needed for the topping and began to sprinkle the red, white and green candy crumbs over the whipped cream which doused the treat.

"Is it a secret?" Rafe chuckled.

"I'll give you a hint. It's got crushed candy canes, and chocolate cookies..."

"Yum!" Dan called out.

She grinned and dipped her fingers into another container on the counter where she'd placed the crushed cookies. She grabbed a handful and sprinkled it on the cream and crushed candy cane.

"And brownies, chocolate pudding and whipped cream."

"Oh, man! JJ, you are killing me here," Rafe laughed.

She'd enjoyed making the delicacy. She'd baked the brownies while Kelly, Blue and the baby had sat in living room and had packed them some so they could take the chocolate treats along with them.

The two women had been so sweet. She'd discovered that Blue and Kelly were best friends. That they worked with several other women pilots on a lake a hundred miles north of Moose Ranch. Envy and an odd urge to break free of her fears had enveloped her as the two women told JJ about the freedom they felt flying above the clouds. They brought mail and food supplies to people who lived in secluded areas of the north. They had government contracts to deliver medical supplies to isolated hospitals. They even flew firefighters deep into the woods to fight forest fires.

The women did so many things and went on so many adventures that JJ had been caught up in their world. It had given her the idea that this ranch needed a bush plane too. And she could be their pilot.

JJ inhaled and rolled her eyes at her silly fantasy. Her? A woman prone to panic and anxiety attacks could never be a bush pilot.

Suddenly, she remembered what Kelly had told her. That she needed to change her way of thinking. Instead of saying she couldn't do something. She needed to believe that she could. Kelly had also confided in JJ that she should know because she'd also suffered from anxiety, panic attacks and agoraphobia when she'd been younger.

If Kelly could become a bush pilot, then JJ needed to believe that yeah, maybe one day she could conquer her fears and be one too.

She smiled and picked up the dessert.

"Okay, guys here it is. Merry Christmas Eve!" she called out.

"Wow! JJ! This is awesome!" Dan said as she presented the trifle to them.

Rafe let out a whoop. He grabbed the spoon and began to heap the dessert onto his plate.

"Hey! Don't take it all!" Dan complained.

"Leave a little for Brady. I need to get the laundry out of the dryer. I'll be back in a minute," she said as she headed toward the mudroom.

Truth was, she needed to see Brady. Where in the world was he? She peeked out a mudroom window into the darkness. A light shone in one of the frost-encrusted barn windows. The guys had said he was tending to a couple of calves that had been born today.

Yet, she wanted him inside. With them. *With her.* Why was she being so possessive? So selfish?

Maybe because she wanted to experience another hot kiss from him. Needed him in her bed tonight. Safe and making love to her. She didn't know how long she stood there staring out the window at that barn door, but finally the light closed and the barn door opened.

Relief rushed through her as Brady stepped outside.

He was safe.

Relief poured through her and she quickly gathered the sheets out of the dryer and placed them in a laundry basket. Before she could grab the basket and head back into the kitchen, the mudroom door opened and frigid air whipped against her as Brady stepped inside.

"Man! It's a cold one out there," he growled as he shut the door behind him. He turned around and smiled when he saw her standing here.

"Hey, are you waiting for me?" His cheeks was flushed red from the cold and his eyes twinkled with amusement.

Had he seen her standing there peering out the window?

"Now, why would I do that? You're a grown man. You don't need me worrying about you."

His smile widened. To her surprise he reached out and grabbed her by her waist, pulling her right against his cold winter clothing. The unmistakeable bulge of an erection pressed boldly against her lower belly.

Oh my! Why is he always so aroused?

"You're damn right I'm a grown man, JJ. And you'll find that out tonight," he said in a deep whisper.

She trembled in his arms and anticipated another kiss. When none came, disappointment rocked her. He studied her with a heated gaze that made her realize he would be more intense than Dan or Rafe. Maybe even more intense than the two of them combined?

Nervousness wiggled through her excitement.

"What size butt plug are you on now?" he asked.

"Large."

He nodded.

"When the guys are asleep tonight, I want you to come to my room." His voice was low and firm, leaving no room for argument.

Numbly, she nodded.

He let her go and then handed her the laundry basket. His eyes blazed with warning as he stared at her.

"Go, before I take you right now up against this wall."

Oh my!

She almost decided to stay just to see if he really would do as he threatened. Almost.

But she wasn't yet comfortable enough for something like that to happen with Rafe and Dan in the other room. Or was she?

She hesitated. Brady's eyes narrowed.

Excitement almost bowled her over.

"Go," he whispered. His voice was a husky demand and her instincts told her he wanted to be alone with her tonight, just as she'd been alone with Rafe and Dan.

She nodded jerkily.

Okay, she would do his bidding. She would wait the next couple of hours and then she'd be with him in his bed. Suddenly nothing else in the world mattered.

Brady clenched his teeth as he watched JJ scurry away with the laundry basket. He'd enjoyed the shock flare in her eyes when he instructed her to come to his room, instead of the way Dan and Rafe had gone to hers.

Feeling her sweet, curvy body pressed against his had instantly made his cock and balls way too tight. It actually pained him to

take the couple of steps to hang up his jacket and other winter
gear.

Man, he needed JJ in a way that he'd never needed any other
woman. He couldn't wait to hear her moaning and crying out as
she'd done last night while Rafe had taken her in that shower.
He'd stood at her bathroom door and for mere seconds he'd
listened to the slaps of flesh against flesh. Knowing she was in
there being fucked by another man, without him watching or
being involved, had made him just about go nuts.

If Kelly hadn't been in trouble, he would have joined Rafe and
JJ in the shower. Without a doubt.

Brady grimaced as he sat down on a chair in the mudroom
and removed his boots. His jeans were too damned tight and his
shaft was too damned swollen. It was going to be torture waiting
to sink his shaft deep into JJ's warm pussy. But it would be worth
the wait. He would endure and it would be much more sweeter
when he came inside of her.

It was silent tonight. Way too quiet, JJ thought as she tiptoed
down the stairway, her arms laden with the Christmas presents
she'd wrapped for the guys. The quiet before the storm, in more
ways than one. At the bottom of the stairs, she stopped to gaze at
the Christmas lights twinkling on the tree and at the windows.

She smiled. Kelly was right. The living room, donned in red
bows, green garland and colorful ornaments, truly did belong in a
magazine. It was breathtaking. But she didn't have the time to
admire it. She needed to get these presents under the tree.

She moved quickly into the living room and smiled to herself
as she placed the presents. The guys would be surprised. She'd
been grateful that Brady hadn't opened any of the sealed boxes
yesterday when he'd brought them into the ranch house. That
had been another reason she'd hadn't had sleep last night.

Excitement at wrapping her purchases had wound her up so much she hadn't been able to do any resting.

She glanced at a clock on the nearby wall. It was almost midnight. Almost Christmas. Not a creature was stirring, not even a cowboy. She gazed around the room again and shook her head. Was she really here? Was she truly, really sincerely here, having sex with three cowboys?

Impatience settled inside her. It was time to go to Brady.

She blew out a tense breathe and stood. Tonight, she wore nothing but a robe. Brady's robe. The same one Kelly had been wearing this morning. But JJ had washed it with the rest of the laundry. The last thing she wanted on Brady or his robe was some other female's scent. She wanted only her smell on his clothes and on him.

A hushed noise from the direction of Brady's bedroom snapped her back to attention. Brady would be waiting for her. Just thinking of the encounter in the mudroom, remembering his heated gaze and that huge bulge pressed against her as he'd held her, promised to bring her plenty of pleasure. That's what she craved. To be held and to feel loved. To lose herself in pleasure, if only for one night.

She took a couple of steps forward and froze. Brady stood right in front of her, not more than three feet away. He wore nothing but his black cowboy hat and black track pants. His arms were crossed over his muscular chest and a sweet smile tilted his lips.

"What are you up to, Mrs. Santa Claus?" he asked as he tried to peek around her.

"Nothing." She giggled as she reached out and grabbed him by his biceps with the intention of pushing him backward and out of the living room so he wouldn't see the presents. Beneath her fingers his muscles flexed, but he was immovable.

"Brady, come on. Please. I don't want you to see," she begged.

"Please what, baby? Why would you have me move from here when all I want to do is see all of you?"

Without waiting for her to reply, he gazed up at the ceiling. She followed his gaze and to her amazement discovered a green plant with a red bow dangling over their heads.

"How in the world did that get there? What was it?"

"Mistletoe."

Mistletoe? No way. This was the first time she'd ever seen mistletoe.

"You know what that means," Brady grinned.

"You're romantic?" she whispered. She couldn't believe it. Brady had put a mistletoe up for her?

"Not a romantic bone in my body, actually," he said with a shake of his head. But his blue eyes glistened with pride.

She held her breath as he unfolded his arms from his chest and lifted his right hand to her robe sash, and undid the tie. Her robe fell open and his hands slid inside and settled upon her waist. His palms were sizzling hot against her flesh and incredibly gentle as he held her...

Heat whipped through her as her gaze moved from his black cowboy hat, to his brilliant blue eyes and locked onto his luscious-looking lips. She ached to kiss him.

Suddenly the grandfather clock nestled in the corner began to clang. She counted twelve times.

Oh my gosh, it was Christmas and she couldn't think of anywhere else she'd rather be than right here.

"Merry Christmas, JJ girl," he whispered.

"Merry Christmas, Brady."

She trembled as he lowered his head and his lips melted over hers. Instantly she was lost inside sweeping sensations as his mouth slid over hers, demanding and delightful.

When he broke the kiss, her knees wobbled and his eyes twinkled as he looked at her.

"I was serious when I told the guys you had me at our first kiss," he said hoarsely. "I hope you don't mind that I divulged that piece of information. It's just whenever I am away from you, you're all I think about, and when I'm near you, I just want to take you to my bed."

JJ swallowed. Wow, what a confession.

He didn't even give her a chance to say she felt the same way about him before suddenly he lifted her into his arms. He held her tightly to his body as if he never wanted to let her go. "I want to make love to you so badly it hurts."

Hot blood coursed through her. Suddenly she wanted his hands all over her. Wanted him fucking her. Making love to her. Professing his undying love to her.

Her breath halted when he carried her into his bedroom. Dozens of tea lights flickered tiny yellow flames. The candles were everywhere. On shelves, on the night tables, on a chair, the dresser and on the windowsills. Delicate Christmas scents of cinnamon and nutmeg drifted beneath her nostrils. She loved the smells, but she loved Brady's scent much more. He smelled of soap and a bit like pine. Like the outdoors. Like freedom.

He set her down on her feet beside the bed and with agonizing slowness he placed his hands on her shoulders and slid the robe off her. The clothing puddled at her feet. An instant of self-conscious awareness pummelled her, but when he slid his track pants down his hips to reveal his engorged arousal, all thoughts of shyness disintegrated.

She swore softly beneath her breath at the size of his cock. His erection was even bigger than Dan's or Rafe's and she shuddered with excitement. A sexual aggressiveness she'd never experienced before lashed her.

She reached up and placed her palms on his hot chest. Soft hairs teased her fingers and hard muscles flexed beneath her finger tips as she pushed him onto the bed. The instant his head hit the pillow, she moved over him, her breasts pillowing against

his chest. She melded her lips over his, quickly reaching a hand
between his thighs and cradled his swollen scrotum. His flesh was
swollen against her palm and she massaged his balls. He groaned
into her mouth and his hands slipped gently against her waist.
Sharp sparks of pleasure tingled along her lips as he kissed her
harder.

Then he surprised her by rolling her over. Suddenly he was on
top and she was beneath him. He broke the kiss and she laughed,
loving how quickly he'd overpowered her. He smiled at her and
his straight teeth gleamed white in the dark. His eyes were dark
and heavy-lidded as he licked his bottom lip.

"I don't know how I survived without you before you came
into my life," Brady whispered.

Her eyes widened at his comment and her mouth dropped
open as to her surprise he produced a bowl from the other side of
his pillow.

"What in the world?" she asked. Curiosity made her grin.

She held her breath while he shuffled his body lower over
hers, until his upper torso and head were between her thighs.
Then he dipped his fingers into the bowl and withdrew chocolate
pudding.

"Ever since you first made us chocolate pudding, this has been
a fantasy of mine," he said tightly.

She laughed but the delight melted into arousal as he sensually
dabbed a dollop of pudding onto her left nipple. The dessert was
cool on her flesh but that didn't last long as Brady quickly
lowered his head, and sucked her chocolate-drenched nipple into
his mouth. Heat enveloped her flesh as he slurped and nibbled.
Sensations, sharp and tight snapped through her and arrowed
right down to her pussy.

He moved quickly to her other breast, smearing pudding over
her tight nipple and then opening his mouth. She watched as her
nipple disappeared between his lips. His tongue stroked her

quivering flesh and with each sharp suck wicked tension mounted inside her.

She blew quick gasps as Brady moved away and began kissing a fiery line over her belly and then lower toward the juncture of her thighs.

Oh my gosh! He was heading south and she was creaming up a storm just thinking about what he was about to do. He removed his cowboy hat and pleasure zapped her as he spread cool chocolate pudding onto her clit. Then his head dipped between her thighs and his mouth melted over her pussy.

Every nerve ending awakened and arousal spiraled through her. His lips slurped on her labia, his tongue darted in and out of her pussy and then his mouth sweetly constricted over her clit. He suckled and sipped until her body stiffened and she couldn't stand the arousal any longer.

She let go. Of her self control. Of her thoughts. Of herself.

She exploded on a shout as the orgasm rocked her. Shudders twisted her hips and she convulsed, her hips thrusting against his face. Her fingers tangled into the bedcovers and she held on as she rode the magnificent waves of pleasure.

As the spasms ebbed, Brady moved his mouth away. The mattress moved and she opened her eyes to find him climbing over her. He was wearing his black cowboy hat again and chocolate pudding lined the edges of his mouth. His gaze was dark with intent and his cock hung heavy and engorged between his thighs.

It looked thick and pulsing. The cock head was flared and wide. She just couldn't seem to take her eyes off it.

She trembled as he eased down on her. His hot damp length covering her, his thick cock head plunging into her wet vagina. Her tense vaginal muscles parted and she struggled to accommodate his thick flesh. When his shaft sunk about two inches into her, he stopped.

She trembled beneath him.

He reached over to her sides and grabbed her wrists, untangling her fingers from the blankets. He intertwined his fingers with hers and and pulled her arms up.

"You are so beautiful," he said as he held her hands hostage above her head and against the mattress.

Her face heated at his compliment and his chocolate-scented breath caressed her mouth.

"I enjoyed the way you were going on down there," she whispered.

He grinned and his eyes twinkled in the candlelight.

"You liked that, did you?" he asked.

"Very much."

His smile disappeared.

"Then by all means, let's continue."

He dipped his head and his lips slid over hers, hard and fierce. His shaft pushed into her vagina, her muscles protesting at the thick girth. A burst of pleasure-pain made her moan, but his kisses shot away her momentary distress.

"What Christmas present did you get me, Ms. Santa?" he whispered after he broke the kiss. He withdrew from her pussy and then thrust slowly into her again, plunging a bit deeper.

She clenched her fingers tighter with his as another bite of pleasure-pain snapped through her. Gosh, but his cock was big and so hard!

"You'll have to fuck the answer out of me," she teased.

"I plan on doing just that," he whispered.

She closed her eyes as he slid his lips over hers again, creating a tingling friction that had her gasping into his mouth.

Her breath caught as he began a faster, much deeper thrust. The hairs on his chest teased her nipples and a rush of arousal burned sharp inside her. His rhythmic lovemaking became fierce and seductive.

Something powerful began to build deep inside her. Her body tightened beneath his. His kisses deepened. Perspiration blossomed over her forehead.

Her hands clenched tightly around his and suddenly she was spiraling. A riptide of pleasure cascaded over her. She went wild, her muscles convulsing, her mind shattering.

She broke the kiss, and cried out as she came.

Brady kept thrusting as shudders rocked her. His hips moved in a quick rhythm and his breaths came faster. His groans grew louder and then suddenly his body went rigid on top of her.

He cried out her name and then his cock pulsed inside her as he joined her in bliss.

JJ's hands were like silk, Brady thought as he watched her sleep. He'd made love to her over and over again through the night and now she lay quietly beside him on the bed. Her closed eyes were framed by long black lashes and a smile that gave him the cutest glimpse of her dimples tipped her mouth.

For the first time in his life, he truly felt sexually satiated. It was crazy because he'd been with a few women and had always thought he'd felt better after a good bout of sex, but with JJ, it was something deep. Something extra-meaningful.

He reached out and pushed a strand of soft, dark hair off her cheek and ran his finger along her chin. So satiny soft. So warm. So beautiful.

To his surprise, his cell phone suddenly rang from somewhere in his room and he remembered leaving his cell in his jean pocket. He'd slung his work jeans over a nearby chair last night while undressing. At first he figured he'd just let it ring, but then JJ stirred. The smile on her face dipped into a frown, but she didn't wake.

Quickly he got out of bed, padded to the chair and dug the cell out of his pocket.

He gazed at the number on the screen. His sister Jenna had finally decided to call him back.

The sound of men laughing dragged JJ from the luscious layers of sleep-drenched dreams about three cowboys making love to her. When she opened her eyes, she knew instinctively that Brady wasn't here with her. She didn't know how she knew it, she just did.

To her surprise, she discovered a white cowboy hat hanging off the headboard bed post right in front of her.

What the heck?

A single red rose and a green-colored card were tied on a red ribbon around the hat brim.

JJ,
This cowgirl hat is for you.
Join us in the living room for more Christmas presents.
Merry Christmas!
Love,
Your Cowboys
Brady, Dan and Rafe

JJ grinned and snuggled deeper beneath the blankets. Her cowboys. Yes, they all belonged to her now. They'd been inside her body and they were inside her heart.

Another round of laughter erupted from the living room and suddenly JJ couldn't wait to be with them.

"JJ, I can't believe that you got us socks, gloves, and scarves that match the color of our cowboy hats," Dan chuckled as he laid out the items she'd given him for Christmas.

Beside him, JJ sat cross-legged, wearing one of Brady's robes. Dan made it a point to get her a romantic red one to wear for them come St. Valentine's Day in February...if she was still here.

His mind wandered to what Jenna had told him this morning. But Dan quickly stomped on it. He didn't want to think about the news she'd brought them. He just wanted to enjoy watching JJ.

Her cheeks were flushed and her eyes glittered as she laughed at his comment. The sweet sound was hearty and came from somewhere deep inside her soul. It made Dan's heart flutter.

"Well, I would have gotten you guys something much more meaningful if I'd had more time. But with chores and you boys popping in at the most inopportune times, I had to be sneaky. Do you know how many times I had to rush out of the office when I heard one of you guys coming in through the mudroom door? I didn't want you guys to catch on that I was getting you Christmas presents."

"Speaking of Christmas presents," Rafe said as he stood.

Brady nodded to the top of the tree and Dan watched JJ follow their gaze. Her brows furrowed as Brady reached up and from behind one of the green branches near the top of the tree, he palmed a small black velvet jewelry box.

Rafe held the box out to her and Dan's heart melted as JJ clutched her hands to her chest.

"For you, JJ. It's from all three of us." Brady said in a thick voice.

Unexpected emotion bubbled inside him as she sucked in her bottom lip and shook her head slowly as if in disbelief.

"You didn't have to get me anything, guys," she said softly. Her cheeks flushed a very pretty pink.

She was embarrassed. Not used to getting things. Well, hell, the three of them would make sure they spoiled her with an abundance of gifts until she stopped blushing and got used to them showering her with presents. Then she'd have other, more intimate reasons to blush.

Dan's breath hitched at that thought. He'd heard her cry out last night when Brady had made love to her. He'd listened to her moans when Rafe had taken her in the shower and he'd experienced those sweet cries while he'd fucked her in her bed.

But when the three of them took her...

He blew out a slow tortured breath as his cock pressed against his track pants. He forced himself to focus on JJ as she reached out. Her fingers were trembling as she accepted the jewelry box.

When she didn't open the box, and simply stared at it, Dan gazed over at Brady who stared back at him and shrugged his shoulders.

"Come on, JJ. Open it. Merry Christmas, sweetheart," Rafe said. He smiled and winked at Dan and Brady.

She shook her head slowly, that look of disbelief still on her face. "You really shouldn't have gotten me anything. I've already got more than I ever deserved."

Was she serious?

"Whoa, baby. You deserve much more than we can ever give you, right, guys?" Dan said. He couldn't believe that she could think such thoughts.

"JJ, girl. We treasure you more than you know," Brady said.

Dan did a double take at Brady's thick voice and in the intense way he studied JJ. Dan had never heard that tone before in the guy. JJ had seriously touched him. Come to think of it, Brady hadn't been grumpy since the day after she'd arrived.

Hell, miracles really did happen. There was hope for the four of them yet!

JJ swore she was going to cry. She didn't own any jewelry. The prison didn't allow inmates to have any. She'd never felt anything so soft before, it was as if the velvet on the box was making love to her fingers.

When she gazed up from the box and saw the exuberance on the men's faces, something wonderful happened inside of her. For the first time in a long time, she realized that she deserved a happily-ever-after, just like anyone else. Disbelief slinked away and belief filled her. Maybe all this was *really permanent*.

She lifted the box lid and her mouth dropped open in surprise. A gorgeous gold necklace twinkled against the velvety white satin interior of the box. On the necklace hung three cowboy hats. Each had a different stone in it.

"The necklace is pure gold," Rafe stated as he lifted the necklace out of the box and held it up for her to see.

The cowboy hats glittered beneath the Christmas tree lights.

"Yeah, and each cowboy hat has a birthstone," Dan said as she watched the cowboy hats dangle on the delicate gold chain.

"The black hat is Brady's. The tiny blue sapphire represents his birthday in September. Rafe's hat is the beige one and yes, that's a real white diamond buried in his. His birthday is in April and the dark-brown hat with the green emerald represents my birthday in May."

"They are all so beautiful." She'd never seen anything so gorgeous. Ever.

"And this came for you just this morning. It was in my email. A hell of a Christmas present," Brady said. He stood and produced a white businesslike envelope from behind the toaster where he'd apparently kept it hidden.

"What is it?"

She frowned as she noticed indecision flood Brady's eyes. Rafe and Dan also had suddenly become incredibly quiet. Weird vibes of uneasiness whispered through the air. She wasn't sure if she liked the solemn expressions on their faces.

Until now the three men had appeared confident and happy to have her around. In the split second that Brady had produced the envelope, they appeared anything but assured.

They almost seemed...scared?

In an instant, the envelope that Brady was holding out to her was the enemy. She didn't want to accept it. Didn't want to know what was in it.

"Before you open it, just know one thing. What is inside doesn't change how we feel about you. We want you to stay here with us. Forever," Brady said softly.

How they felt about her? What in the world was Brady talking about?

The words forever rang through her mind and she bit back a flood of emotion.

"What, pray tell, would be in the envelope that would change the way I feel about you guys?" There was no way anything would make her feel any differently than she did about them. She needed them in her life. She cared about them. She loved them.

She shook her head. "I don't want it. Just toss it."

Brady looked stunned. Rafe and Dan frowned.

"JJ, you are going to want to see what is in that envelope," Dan soothed.

"Why are you guys looking so gloomy? It's Christmas, and presents are supposed to make us happy. This envelope is giving me bad vibes," she admitted.

What had up until now been the best Christmas of her life was quickly turning not so nice.

"Believe us, you are going to want to see what's inside, baby," Dan said. To her surprise, he slung an arm over her shoulders and squeezed gently.

"You need to open this. It's the best Christmas present ever," Brady replied. He sat down on the floor beside JJ and put the envelope in her lap. His smile was wobbly. He continued to be uncertain. But why? What was in the envelope?

"If it's the best, then why the frowns?" she asked.

"We're afraid you'll want to leave us," Brady said. His gaze was shuttered. A muscle twitched in his cheek.

Irritation whipped through her.

"Why are you guys being so damned mysterious?"

To her surprise, all three of them laughed.

"You're the one that's mysterious in not opening the envelope, JJ," Rafe said with a chuckle.

JJ stared at the envelope in her lap. Her full name, Jennifer Jane Watson, was written on it. Not JJ. It was Brady's handwriting. But why had he written her name so formally?

She swallowed at her suddenly dry throat. Her heart began an incredibly fast thump against her chest. The inklings of anxiety sparked at the back of her mind.

Shit. Not now. She couldn't have an attack now.

She needed to know what was inside. She had to know what was making them so uneasy.

She took a deep breath and tore open one end of the sealed envelope. A folded sheet of paper was inside. With shaky fingers, she plucked out the paper and unfolded it.

The letter looked official. She read the typed words as if she were mesmerized. But three words made the biggest impact on her.

Criminal Record Suspension. Otherwise known as a pardon.

She could barely hear Brady as he spoke.

"My sister called me this morning. She forwarded the letter here via email and I printed it out for you. She knows people who know people and they reviewed your sentence. Jenna said that you had a poor defense lawyer and there were so many openings for appeals and dismissals that it wasn't even funny. She said you should never have gone to prison based on the self-defence wounds on your arms and hands and other areas on your body. And that you had every right to defend yourself based on his past behavior toward your mother and you."

Oh damn. The guys knew all the details? That when she'd come home from visiting a friend, she'd found her mother's dead body in the hallway and she'd lost her mind. She'd confronted her step-father while he'd casually sat watching tv. He'd, acted as if her dead mother wasn't even in the house. As if he hadn't killed her.

He'd been irritated at being disturbed by her screaming and had started beating on JJ. She'd suffered a broken arm, a broken wrist and in her fear for her life, as well as her rage against him for what he'd done to her mother, she'd grabbed the fireplace poker and smashed the metal bar over the head with it, killing him instantly. Seeing him go down the way he had, had brought instant relief and happiness pouring through her. She'd said as much to the cops who'd shown. Cops, who'd been his co-workers and they'd made sure she paid for what she'd done to that son-of-a-bitch.

"They looked at your good behavior in prison as well, and her friends were able to get the appropriate people to get you a pardon. She emailed this just this morning. The pardon is legit," Brady said softly.

"Congratulations, JJ," both Rafe and Dan said.

Now they sounded cheerful, but she could barely hear them from the rush of disbelief buzzing through her ears.

She'd been pardoned? She was free?

"You're shaking," Dan said as he hugged her close to him. His warm embrace was just what she needed and she melted into his strength.

"I...I don't know what to say?" she said as she stared at the paper.

"A hell of a Christmas present I'd say. We are very excited for you, JJ." Rafe winked.

"You're free, JJ, girl," Brady said with a grin.

Doubt rocked her. She was free. So why did she not feel that way?

Suddenly the lights overhead flickered. Then the house dropped into darkness.

Oh crap. Not again.

"JJ is being too damned quiet," Rafe shouted from behind Brady as they both stumbled through the snowdrifts. They were using the guide rope so they wouldn't get lost in the blizzard as they headed toward the ranch house from the barn.

Howling wind froze the skin on his face and stinging snowflakes bit painfully into his cheeks. The cold urged him to move faster, but he couldn't pick up the pace because the snow was piling quickly and reaching past his knees. It appeared there would be no relief from this storm anytime soon.

After a quick lunch, they'd spent a good portion of the afternoon checking on the nervous cattle in the barn. Dan had helped him deliver two calves this afternoon. Christmas calves. Both had been difficult births, but the calves were sturdy and healthy. Their mothers, despite being weak from birthing, had taken to their newborns immediately.

The cows reminded him of JJ. When she had kids, she would be just like the new mothers. Protective, nurturing and loving. She was like that with them. A sexy mother hen. A woman who naturally loved to take care of people.

Through the Freedom Run program, they'd been given some information about JJ's brutal past, and that's why they hadn't pushed her about details about her incarceration. When she'd admitted it was just her in the world with no family, it had only endeared her to them that much more.

Now she was free to leave them.

His gut twisted with sadness.

"I wasn't expecting her reaction to that pardon. She didn't crack a smile. Hadn't seemed happy. She'd been happier with the necklace. What was up with that?" Brady shouted.

"I don't have a clue. I just know that I don't like seeing her upset. It kills me," Rafe shouted back.

"Any suggestions as to what we should do to cheer her up?"

"If a pardon doesn't make a woman happy, then hell if I know what will!" Rafe replied.

The two of them fell silent and as they neared the ranch house a figure loomed out of the swirling snow right in front of them.

It was Dan. His arms were laden with firewood. His eyebrows and cheeks were white with snow.

"Hell of a storm, eh?" Dan shouted.

"A good one!" Brady yelled back.

Rafe scrambled up the snow covered stairs first and shoved the door open so they could get out of the blustery wind.

"Hey, smells nice in here. JJ says she's making turkey for Christmas dinner," Dan said as Brady grabbed pieces of wood and placed it quickly on the existing pile just inside the door.

"I can smell gingerbread cookies, too. One of my favorites," Rafe grinned.

"Mine too. I'm guessing that's why she kicked me out. So she could surprise us with the cookies," Dan chuckled as the three of them removed the gloves and hats that JJ had given them as presents and then took off their coats and then hung them on nearby hooks. They kicked off their boots and quickly stuffed them along the wall out of the way.

"Firewood should be enough to hold us through the night. It took me more than a freaking hour just to get all this wood inside. You probably didn't notice that I shoveled a walkway to the barn, but by the time I was finished I had to shovel my way back to the ranch house," Dan laughed.

"Hell, if you hadn't, we probably would still be trying to get through," Rafe grinned.

Brady inhaled the aroma of turkey and baking deep into his lungs and let the memories sink into him. Christmas back home when he'd been a kid in Toronto had always been an exciting time. His mom, a part-time high school teacher, baked up a storm around Christmas. She'd get them all singing Christmas songs, have them put on aprons and she'd teach them to bake fruitcakes and cookies. Dad, a successful architect, always took care of cooking a couple of huge turkeys.

It had been a good life. Really good. And then one day it had just vanished.

A frisson of sadness whispered through Brady as he remembered his parents were no longer around. They'd died five years ago, shortly after Christmas. Dad's car had slid on an ice patch on the way to the family cottage north of Toronto. The car had done a donut and stalled right in the middle of the major highway. A transport truck had smashed right into them. Both of his parents had died upon impact. His youngest sister, Ginny, had been in the car and had suffered serious injuries. Thankfully, though, she'd survived.

"Where are those gingerbread cookies?" Rafe yelled as he rubbed his hands together and led the way down the hallway.

When they entered the kitchen, JJ wasn't there. But they were greeted to a heaping pile of gingerbread cookies on a plate set upon the dining room table. The cookies looked delicious. JJ had decorated them with wisps of white frosting, giving each gingerbread eyes and a smiling mouth.

To his surprise, something was set right beside the cookies. A small red wicker basket with a huge red bow on the handle.

"What the hell?" Dan whispered as he and Rafe stood beside Brady and peered inside the basket.

"Who left that there?" Rafe asked.

"Who do you think?" Dan chuckled.

Brady blinked in surprise as he stared at the large tube of lube, packages of colorful condoms and sexy, see-through black panties.

"There's a note," Dan said. Before Dan could grab the note, Brady plucked it out of the basket.

The turkey can keep.

What will it be?

The gingerbread men, or me with three?

"Me with three? What does..." Rafe's words trailed off.

"Light-bulb moment," Dan whispered.

"Shit," Brady replied as the full meaning of her note and the contents of the basket hit home.

JJ was ready. For all three of them.

JJ knew the instant the men found her note and the basket. One moment they'd been downstairs talking and laughing, and the next moment silence permeated the ranch house. Supper wouldn't be ready for a couple more hours and she'd left her panties in the basket. She wore the white cowboy hat they'd given her and she also wore a black see-through negligee that left little to their imagination. She'd purchased it online and it had come with their presents.

The instant she'd seen that gown, she'd known it was for her. For her sexy side. The side she wanted to experiment with, considering all she'd been able to do in prison was masturbate. And it had been halfhearted because of the cameras.

What she wore wasn't the only clothing she'd purchased. She'd bought necessities, such as better-fitting jeans, tops, and something she'd always wanted but had never felt the need to have while in prison—makeup.

She'd put on just a swipe of pink lipstick and some black mascara. She liked her new look. She hoped the guys would like it too.

She trembled with both fear and excitement as she stared out her bedroom window. Swirls of snow pelted the glass pane and tumbled over the nearby meadow and the yard. But beyond that, she couldn't see anything except fresh and clean white. Everything far away was just...not there.

It was like her life right now. She couldn't see beyond today, because things had changed so dramatically this morning when Brady had handed her the envelope containing her future.

Her entire stay here had been fraught with disbelief at how lucky she'd been. At first to get paroled, and then to come here and meet three easygoing cowboys who'd taken her in even when they'd expected other people for the job. They had bedded her. They had told her she was family.

Now, with the pardon, she owed Brady's sister big time for doing all that she'd done. Jenna had opened a door to JJ's future. Now she was free to do whatever she wanted. Yet as much as things had changed, everything was still the same.

She wanted to stay here with them. She needed Brady, Rafe and Dan, and they needed her to take care of them and to love them. The three men had so easily buried themselves inside her heart, and now she wanted all three of them buried inside her body.

A soft noise at the door made her turn around.

The guys stood there. Brady holding the red basket, and Rafe and Dan standing behind him. They each wore their cowboy hats. No shirts. No shoes. No socks. Just a whole lot of muscles and jeans. Jeans with huge bulges at the juncture of their thighs.

Aroused nervousness shot through her. Their eyes were dark and heavy-lidded. They stared at her as if she was their prey. As if they wanted to devour her. She could hear them too. They were breathing heavily. Their need to dominate her drifted through the air and wrapped around her.

Her breasts suddenly felt heavy. Her legs melted with weakness. Lust pulsed through her, thick and heavy. She creamed.

Oh my gosh, what had she unleashed in writing that note and leaving that basket on the table? She'd done it on impulse. Had wanted a ménage for her Christmas present.

Her hands knotted nervously as Brady stepped forward and placed the basket at the foot of her bed. Then he prowled toward her. His legs were long and he walked with confidence. That bulge between his thighs seemed much larger now.

He reached out his hands and took hers. He squeezed her fingers gently as if to reassure her that she'd made the right choice. But had she?

Suddenly, she was terrified. Doubt cascaded through her as Brady let go of her hands. His fingers dropped to his jeans.

"You look fantastic in black," he whispered as he unzipped his pants.

She began to shake. She bit her bottom lip and watched as his cock jerked free. It angled straight up toward his belly. It was thick and swollen. Very big.

"I'm going to enjoy watching you get taken by the three of us, JJ, girl," he whispered.

Her pussy trembled with exquisite heat.

Behind Brady she could hear the rustling of clothing. Rafe and Dan were undressing and when Brady moved aside, she saw their erections, jerking as they stroked themselves.

She blew out a tense breath as Rafe stalked over to her and then behind her.

"Lube," he called out.

Dan grabbed the lube from the basket and tossed it to Rafe, who caught it with ease. Then Dan joined Brady and stood beside him in front of her. Dan's appreciative stare lingered on her breasts and then lifted to capture JJ's gaze.

"Brady is right, JJ. You look fantastic. You are absolutely glowing," Dan whispered.

Dan nudged past Brady and stepped closer. She held her breath as he grabbed her hands and held them in much the same way as Brady had just done. His fingers gently squeezed hers.

"We hadn't expected that you would be ready so soon," Dan said. His eyes glittered with appreciation and he smiled tightly.

"I...I'm not sure I am," she whispered, telling him the truth. But her body was humming with an intense anticipation that she'd never experienced before. She liked it.

"You are. Or you wouldn't have left us that note, the basket or the lube," Brady said.

She swallowed and nodded jerkily. He was right.

"Rafe will prepare you while Dan and I play with you," Brady whispered.

"O...okay."

She worried her bottom lip as the slurp of lube echoed through the air.

"Yeah, we'll give you something to remember us by." Dan slid his hand along the outside of her upper thigh. His fingers were hot and created a tingling line of pleasure.

Suddenly, she understood why the men had looked so forlorn when the envelope with her pardon had been presented to her. They thought they had lost her. That she would grab the pardon and take off.

"But I don't want to leave," she whispered.

All three of them stiffened. Oh no. She'd said something wrong.

"Unless...you don't want me to stay," she breathed. Insecurity rushed through her. What if they didn't want her to stay?

Behind her Rafe swore softly beneath his breath. Brady and Dan stared at her as if she suddenly had sprouted horns out of her head.

"Baby, are you serious? We wouldn't be fucking you if we didn't want you," Dan said.

He smiled and his hands settled on her waist, his touch was a pleasant burn on her skin. He leaned in and his breath was hot against the side of her neck. Bristles from his chin tickled her skin as he sucked her earlobe into his mouth. He nibbled until sweet shimmers whispered up and down her neck. When he drew his face away, JJ wanted him back there.

"We want you to stay with us forever," Brady whispered.

He grinned and his cheeks darkened with a slight blush. That shy look that she'd noticed her first night here showed up again. Her heart fluttered. That expression on his face was so endearing.

"More than forever," Rafe growled from behind her.

Wow, they sounded so possessive. Exquisite happiness exploded in her heart. She really belonged here. Belonged to them.

She sucked in a breath as a heavily lubed finger slid against her tight sphincter. She'd removed the largest plug this morning after a quick shower and she'd been feeling empty down there ever since. Now, with Rafe pressing his finger into her ass, her muscles eagerly clenched at the intrusion. He pressed his finger past the ring of muscles and she hissed as he slid it in deeper.

In front of her, Dan's hand settled onto the hem of her negligee and she held her breath as he lifted the material to expose her pussy and then her breasts.

"Lift your arms, baby," Dan whispered. She did as he asked and he slid the negligee up over her head, and then dropped the filmy garment upon on the floor. She was naked, fully exposed to them. But she didn't have time to be shy as Dan dipped his head. He cupped her breasts and sucked her nipple right into his hot mouth. She moaned at the exquisite pressure as he nibbled and lapped.

Brady had angled his body to her right side. His fingers touched her chin, urging her to turn her head toward his. When she did, his lips caught hers in a searing kiss that sent shockwaves straight down to her toes. His tongue boldly pushed into her mouth and he began stroking her tongue. Sensations shimmied up and down her spine. His kiss was intense and addictive. Needing more, she moved closer to his body, her hands sliding around his engorged shaft.

His cock jerked against her palms and he groaned into her mouth. His kiss intensified.

Behind her, Rafe withdrew his finger. The slurp of lube followed and she gasped into Brady's mouth as Rafe inserted two slippery fingers. Her thighs clenched as he pushed his fingers deeper into her. Pressure snapped against her anal muscles. The sensations excited her.

He withdrew his fingers again. The slurp of lube followed and her knees weakened as he pressed three fingers into her. The thickness of the intrusion made her heady. Made her want his cock sliding in and out of her.

She moaned and widened her legs, needing more stimulation. She twisted her palms around Brady's cock. It twitched and throbbed in her hands.

Dan moved his head to her other breast and sucked her other nipple into his mouth. She gasped as his hard shaft burned along the side of her thigh. The pressure of his lips on her nipple drove her wild. Every muscle in her body tensed. Suddenly she just couldn't wait anymore. A sense of urgency made her break the kiss.

"Now! Take me now," she hissed against Brady's mouth.

Suddenly, the three men moved in unison and they led her to her bed. Condom packages were ripped open. Cocks sheathed with protection.

Brady lay down close to the edge of the bed, his cock spearing into the air. He held out his arms to her and suddenly she couldn't wait to mount him. She scrambled onto the bed.

Onto him.

He grabbed her hips as she climbed over him. The thick bulge of his cock head nudged past her labia and pushed into her vagina, stretching her muscles and making her moan at the incredible pressure. Within a second, she was fully impaled. Her pussy gripped the intrusion and her muscles clasped around him.

Brady groaned and his hands tightened on her hips. She began to gyrate against his shaft, loving the hot fullness buried inside her.

To her right, Dan stood at the side of the bed.

"Look this way, baby. Take me into your sweet mouth," he hissed.

Brady helped to angle her upper body closer to the edge of the bed and then she opened her mouth, eager to accept Dan's cock.

"Spread your thighs for me, sweetheart." Rafe's command was strangled, desperate. Quickly she widened her legs, eager for him to take her.

Everything was happening so fast. Behind her, the cheeks of her ass were pulled apart. She moaned around Dan's flesh as Rafe's cock head nudged against her sphincter. Immediately she understood why he'd lubed her so much. He entered easily and stretched her hole. Her tight ring of muscles instantly spasmed against the intrusion and her pussy clenched around Brady's shaft.

The guys were moaning and groaning now. Rafe withdrew and thrust into her ass, making her burn. Her lips tightened around Dan's thick member. She'd never had a man's penis in her mouth before, but she followed her instincts, licking and sucking his scorching length and listening to his grunts of appreciation.

She keened as Rafe's thrusts increased in speed, pushing her closer to the climax she craved. With every buck of his hips, he pressed her harder against Brady, her ultra-sensitive clit stimulated by Brady's pelvic bone. Brady groaned as her vagina tightened like a vise around his thickening flesh. Her ass greedily hugged Rafe's penis.

Wicked sensations arced into her.

The sounds of flesh slapping against flesh mingled with her moans and their groans. It was a musical rhythmic pulsating noise that burrowed deep into her senses. Sharp and hot pleasure exploded and tore through her.

She was airborne. All self-control was lost as she writhed on Brady's cock, her hips bucking, her ass and pussy spasming around the thick intruders.

Such sweet pleasure. Such deep, mind-wrenching sensations.

She was lost. She was loved. She was *home*.

The End

Newsletter

Hi! If you would like to get an email when my books are released, you can sign up here:

Newsletter: http://ymlp.com/xguembmugmgb

Your emails will never be shared and you can unsubscribe whenever you like.

For more ebooks and print books please visit http://www.janspringer.com

Want more Jan Springer Adult Romances?

Mini Catalog

Kidnap Fantasies Series

In the land of the rich and famous, the top-secret Kidnap Fantasies is the answer to discreet and naughty downtime.

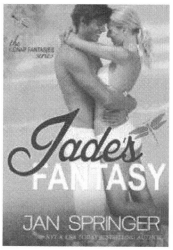

Book One
Jade's Fantasy
When ex-downhill skier Jade's two sisters give her a Kidnap Fantasies questionnaire, Jade is aroused at the prospect of having no-strings fun in the sun with a stranger whose only job would be to fulfill her every intimate fantasy. Although she knows she's too

shy to send it in, she secretly pours her deepest wishes into the questionnaire.

Soon the questionnaire mysteriously vanishes and Jade's fantasy man appears on her luxury yacht in the form of a sexy handy man who gives her an intimate toy-filled holiday she'll never forget.

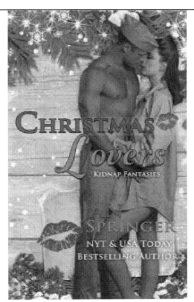

Book Two
Christmas Lovers
(can also be found in the Merry Ménage Kisses Boxed Set)
Sergeant Connor Jordan, wounded overseas and sent back to the States to recuperate, just cannot stop fantasizing about the sexy nurse who cared for him. When his brothers give him a holiday gift certificate to Kidnap Fantasies, a top-secret fantasy organization, Connor knows he'll use their gift, if only to help him forget his wickedly delicious attraction to Nurse Sparks.

Nurse Tania Sparks has always been purely professional with her injured soldiers...until sinfully sexy Connor Jordan enters her hospital. He makes her body throb with an intense desire she's never known before. The last thing she wants is to get involved with the injured warrior. So what's a woman supposed to do to relieve her naughty frustrations? Call Kidnap Fantasies and have them supply her with a look-alike man who'll help her forget her sexy soldier...

When Tania and Connor unexpectedly come together at a secluded mountain chalet, their love explodes in a ménage of passion, sensuous desires and a happily forever after.

Contains ménage scenes.

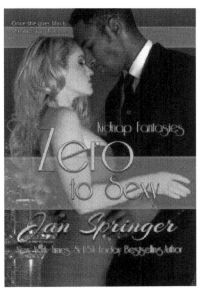

Book Three
Zero to Sexy

Because Santana hides from something bad in his past he lives
only for the moment and doesn't dare dream of a future. He
exists within the sensual world of Kidnap Fantasies, a top-secret
escort world where he explores his sexuality and enjoys pleasure
with both men and women.

But it is love at first sight the instant he sees Amy at his good
friend's wedding. She's got future written all over her. He knows
she is a hunger he must deny, so why is he whispering "you're
mine" to her at the wedding?

The instant Amy Sparks sees the handsome African American at her sister's wedding, she knows in her heart that he's everything she's ever fantasized about in a lover, but before they can connect, he mysteriously disappears. Upon discovering he works for Kidnap Fantasies, she knows how he'll make all her intimate fantasies come true...

When Santana's next Kidnap Fantasies assignment turns out to be Amy, he knows he must protect her from his past and he can be with her only this one time...

Reader Advisory: Includes a sizzling ménage scene and some male on male sensual interaction.

Boxed Sets

***SIX Erotic Romance Ménage Stories! INCLUDES A
BONUS MÉNAGE EBOOK***

BONUS Ménage BOOK "Cowboys for Christmas" book 1 of Jan's new Cowboys Online series. Jennifer Jane is getting THREE Cowboys for Christmas ~ What more could a girl want?

Jennifer Jane Watson has spent the past ten Christmases in a maximum-security prison. The last thing she expects is to get early parole along with a job on a secluded Canadian cattle ranch serving Christmas holiday dinners to three of the sexiest cowboys she's ever met!

Step into The Key Club's Ménage Nights where naughty fantasies come true and two men are hotter than one. Includes FIVE bestselling The Key Club stories; Ménage, Marley's Ménage, A Merry Ménage Christmas, Sophie's Ménage and Jewel's Ménage.

The Key Club Series

Ménage - Book One

Sandwiched between constant deadlines, erotic romance author, Claire Miller, enjoys an occasional unwind at The Key Club...this time she's going to indulge in a yummy ménage.

Marley's Ménage - Book Two

Single soon-to-be mom Marley Madison has had some wicked
cravings in her day, but being pregnant has made her cravings
downright...naughty. She wants a sizzling ménage and she needs
it bad.

A Merry Ménage Christmas - Book Three

Dr. Kelsie Madison can't remember the last time she's had no-strings sex and that's her clue she's been working way too hard. It's time to unwind at the Key Club by indulging in a yummy Christmas present for herself...a red-hot ménage.

Sophie's Ménage - Book Four

It's Spank-Me Ménage Night at the Key Club and Sophie is finally taking the plunge back into the spank scene...she didn't expect her two ex-boyfriends to be there too.

Jewel's Ménage - Book Five

She thought she would never trust a man again...
Until one rainy night two hunky truckers come to Jewel's
rescue, igniting delicious desires for a red-hot ménage a trios.

Jaxie's Ménage - Book Six

A close encounter with death pushes Jaxie into making one of her most intimate fantasies come true...

A Homecoming Ménage Christmas - Book Seven

Rachel has a very naughty secret and she's way too embarrassed to let anyone know about it. When The Key Club throws a Santa Fetish Ménage Night, it's almost too good to be true. She has to figure out how to participate without anyone finding out!

Pleasure Bound Box Set
The Complete Series
Books 1 - 6

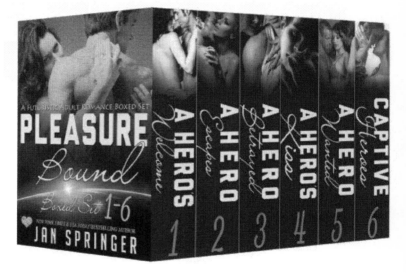

A Futuristic Adult Romance
Books 1-6

This PLEASURE BOUND BOXED SET is an EROTIC ROMANCE and includes the first SIX books in the Pleasure Bound series.

TOP-SECRET MISSION: Explore a recently discovered planet in outer space.

DISCOVERY: A sizzling trip into the realms of bondage, bdsm, pleasure-pain, betrayal and...love.

Inside this Boxed Set:
During a top-secret mission to a newly discovered planet, the six Hero siblings are thrust into a sensual world of erotic violence, unconventional romance and sizzling sex.

A HERO'S WELCOME

Pleasure Bound Book One
Jan Springer
Being shot and held captive isn't what astronaut Joe Hero had in mind when he agreed to a top-secret mission to explore a newly discovered planet for NASA.
But a man would have to be dead not to fall for the sensual female doctor in charge of his care.
One night of scorching passion in the arms of the stranger from another planet is enough to convince Dr. Annie there's more to males than she's been taught by the Educators.
Who is this sexy hunk and why does she welcome him into her bed and her heart *every* chance she gets?

A HERO ESCAPES

Pleasure Bound Book Two
Jan Springer
Queen Jacey has always fantasized about bedding a male.
But taking one for her enjoyment is strictly forbidden. That
is, until an attractive well-hung stranger from another planet
forces her to overcome her training and her beliefs.
Being held captive and forced to mate with a gorgeous Queen
isn't exactly what astronaut Ben Hero expected when he agreed
to explore a newly discovered planet for NASA.
Escaping *should* be his top priority but making sizzling love to
Jacey *is* all he can think about.
When he discovers she's also being held captive, Ben's
protective instincts kick in big time.
Suddenly they're on the run, irresistibly aroused, and wrapped
in each other's arms every chance they get!

A HERO BETRAYED

Pleasure Bound Book Three
Jan Springer

Astronaut Buck Hero didn't count on being held captive or becoming infected with passion poison when he agreed to explore a newly discovered planet for NASA.

If he doesn't get the cure soon he's going to be one *very* dead man.

Fugitive on-the-run Virgin has just rescued an infected male and needs to administer the cure - a twenty-four-hour sex marathon. Then she'll turn him over to his enemies in order to gain her freedom.

But her well-laid plans go into orbit when she discovers she's fallen in love with the stranger from another world.

A HERO'S KISS

Pleasure Bound Book Four
Jan Springer
*During a secret NASA mission to locate their brothers on the
faraway planet of Paradise, the Hero sisters become separated after
they crash land...and find unexpected romance with the tormented
male warriors of the species.*

Jarod and Piper

Being injured and infected by sensuous swamp water isn't what Piper Hero signed up for when she agreed to search for her three missing brothers. But when she's rescued by a dangerously sexy man who makes her so hot that she can't even think straight, Piper is glad that she came.

Jarod Ellis has sworn off women. But he's captivated by Piper Hero, a woman who claims to be related to the Earthmen he has vowed to protect with his life. Although he mistrusts her, she sets free a carnal inferno of needs he's never experienced during his previous life as a pleasure slave.

Despite her intimate fantasies coming true, Piper knows she needs to continue her mission of reuniting her siblings and she'll do it-with or without the help of her well-hung stud...

A HERO WANTED

Pleasure Bound Book Five
(Loosely connected with this series)
Jan Springer
Old-fashioned gal needs a man who loves to walk in the rain.
Must be well-hung. A homebody, white picket fence-type of guy.
Sexual requirements-gentle yet untamed lover. He must be sexually
adventurous who will train me to be same. Must be romantic, enjoy
toys, interested in mutual light bondage, ménages are welcome.
That's what full-figured, antiques shop owner Jenna MacLean
wants when she and her best friend outline a want ad just for fun
on their weekly girls' night out.
After years of being away from his pretty-plus sized ex-
girlfriend, Sully's back in town. When he finds the want ad, he
knows he's the only man who can make all of Jenna's sizzling-hot
fantasies come true.
She's never left his heart and he needs her back in his bed-but
he's not going the traditional romantic route. This time, he'll
prove he loves her with help from the notorious Ménage Club, a
relationship club designed specifically to get estranged couples
back together with the help of a third and sometimes a fourth in
the bedroom.

CAPTIVE HEROES

Pleasure Bound Book Six
Jan Springer
*During a secret NASA mission to locate their brothers on the
faraway planet of Paradise, the Hero sisters become separated after
they crash land...and find unexpected romance with the tormented
alien male warriors of the species in this ultra-long scifi book.*

Taylor and Kayla

While searching for her brothers, Kayla Hero is bound and imprisoned by the Breeders— along with a male captive whose tantalizing scars pique her interest. Forced to escape with him, she's irresistibly aroused when she suddenly becomes *his* captive. Wild lust flares in Kayla's eyes— a sensual side effect of the Fever Swamp water she's accidentally ingested. Taylor knows he will enjoy administering the cure — lots of sizzling hot lovemaking!

Blackie and Kinley

Injured and lost in a dense jungle, Kinley Hero is intimidated by the scarred man who hunts her, especially due to the power of erotic submission he holds over her.

Capturing his beautiful female prey, Blackie can't wait to train her as a pleasure slave for the Death Valley Boys. When her captor slips a collar around her neck, Kinley must struggle with lust as a natural submissive.

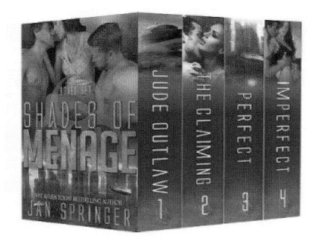

Shades of Ménage Boxed Set: Four Book Romance Ménage Collection

A fast-acting virus has killed a majority of the world's female population. Women's rights are stripped away and The Claiming Law is created, allowing groups of men to stake a claim on a female—as their sensual property.

After five years of fighting in the Terrorist Wars, the Outlaw brothers are coming home to declare ownership on the women they love...and they'll do it any way they can in **Jude Outlaw and The Claiming**.

PLUS

In the future...for population control, each human is embedded with a microchip that suppresses the urge to mate.

*Centuries later,...*A rebel group of young doctors are secretly tampering with their microchips and experimenting with intimacy. Now they search for allies who can help them with their cause – to eventually free humanity in the Dystopian Romance Ménage stories **"Perfect" & "Imperfect"**.

A CONTEMPORARY EROTIC ROMANCE BOXED SET
Naughty Girl Desires Boxed Set: Romance, Contemporary Romance, Romance Suspense, Box Set (m/f only)

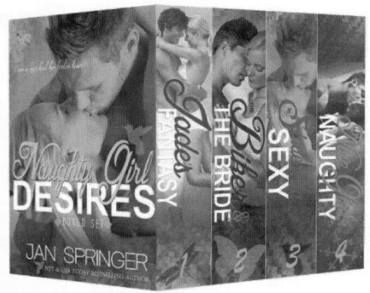

What You'll Find Inside Naughty Girl Desires
Jade's Fantasy
Kidnap Fantasies 1
Jan Springer

In the land of the rich and famous, Kidnap Fantasies is the answer to discreet naughty downtime.

When ex-downhill skier Jade Hart's two sisters give her a Kidnap Fantasies questionnaire, Jade is aroused at the prospect of having no-strings fun in the sun with a stranger whose only job would be to fulfill her every intimate fantasy. Although she knows she's too shy to send it in, she secretly pours her deepest wishes into the questionnaire.

Soon the questionnaire mysteriously vanishes and Jade's fantasy man appears on her luxury yacht in the form of a sexy handy man who gives her an intimate toy-filled Christmas holiday she'll never forget.

The Biker and The Bride

Jan Springer

Wrapped in red-hot lust for revenge, Avery plots to murder the man responsible for the death of her son. Her plans are dashed when her ex-husband crashes her wedding and whisks her away on his motorcycle to the rustic Canadian wilderness cabin they'd once honeymooned.

Police detective, Mason is fighting for Avery's love with everything he has.

Armed with whipped cream, handcuffs and his undying devotion, Mason vows he will make Avery love again. But it's only a matter of time before the man she'd planned to kill hunts them down...

Sinderella Sexy

Jan Springer

By day, she's a dedicated gynecologist.
*By night, Dr. Ella Cinder, escapes reality by secretly performing
in her own erotic, adult version of Cinderella, aptly re-titled
Sinderella.*

When sexy colleague Dr. Roarke Stephenson shows up in the
Sinderella audience on the same night her Prince Charming
stands her up, Ella seizes the opportunity to make Roarke into
her Prince Charming for one carnal night of extremely naughty
fun in front of an audience.

But at the strike of midnight, Ella knows she must face the
harsh reality that Roarke must never learn her secret life and they
can never be together again. Until then, she'll make sure he'll
never forget their night of sensual play.

Dr. Roarke Stephenson is immediately captured by the
lusciously curvy actress who hides behind a mask and is known
only as Sinderella. For some insane reason she reminds him of his
klutzy co-worker, Ella. But that's not possible. Ella would never
have the nerve to do the wickedly delicious things Sinderella does
to him, or would she?

Nice Girl Naughty

Jan Springer

Blind since nineteen, Summer has blossomed into a famous
wood carver. When she's almost killed by a serial killer, she's
whisked away to a secluded wilderness cabin by the man she once
secretly loved.

Summer can't get enough of touching professional bodyguard
Nick Cassidy's thick, powerful muscles and all those other hard,
yummy male body parts that she has always longed to explore.

For years Nick has stayed away from his best friend's kid
sister, nice girl Summer. Now he's back, and sweeping his
gorgeous redhead into the naughty cravings he's always had for
her. With passion blinding him, Nick doesn't realize their
hideout isn't safe—until it's too late.

Please note: The titles in Naughty Girl Desires have been
previously published.

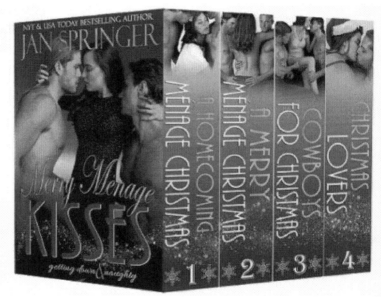

What You'll Find In The
Merry Ménage Kisses Boxed Set
Wrap yourself in four sexy holiday themed adult romance
ménages.

A Homecoming Ménage Christmas

Jan Springer

Rachel has a *very* naughty secret and she's way too embarrassed to let anyone know about it. When The Key Club throws a Santa Fetish Ménage Night it's almost too good to be true. She *has* to figure out how to participate without anyone finding out!

Key Club bartenders Rob and Ron Simpson have fallen head over Santa hats for quiet, nice girl Rachel. But she has no clue how they feel about her. But she *will* know, because Rachel is coming home from a trip to Europe and the twin brothers are going to give her the best Homecoming Ménage Christmas ever. They'll do it with the help of some naughty toys, the Red Room, a safe word and...Santa Claus.

A Merry Ménage Christmas

Jan Springer

Dr. Kelsie Madison can't remember the last time she's had no-strings sex and that's her clue she's been working way too hard. It's time to unwind at the Key Club by indulging in a yummy Christmas present for herself. Something she's never experienced before - a red-hot ménage.

ER Dr. Ryder Greene and his roommate, physiotherapist, Dixon Flynn love sharing their women. They've had their eye on cute Dr. Kelsie Madison for quite some time, but she's a workaholic and she never has time to play.

When they learn she'll be at the Santa Claus Ménage Night festivities, they'll make sure they're the ones kissing Kelsie under the mistletoe. And if they get their wish, Kelsie will be taking them home for Christmas.

Cowboys for Christmas

Jan Springer

Jennifer Jane (JJ) Watson has spent the past ten Christmases in a maximum-security prison.

The last thing she expects is to get early parole, along with a job on a remote Canadian cattle ranch serving Christmas holiday dinners to three of the sexiest cowboys she's ever met!

Rafe, Brady and Dan thought they were getting a couple of male ex-cons to help out around their secluded ranch, but instead they get an attractive and very appealing female.

In the snowbound wilds of Northern Ontario, female companionship is rare.

It's a good thing the three men like to share...

They're dominating, sexy-as-sin and they fill JJ with the hottest ménage fantasies she's ever had. Suddenly she's craving cowboys for Christmas and wishing for something she knows she can never have...a happily ever after.

Christmas Lovers

Jan Springer

Sergeant Connor Jordan, wounded overseas and sent back to the States to recuperate, just cannot stop fantasizing about the sexy nurse who cared for him. When his brothers give him a holiday gift certificate to Kidnap Fantasies, a top-secret fantasy organization, Connor knows he'll use their gift, if only to help him forget his wickedly delicious attraction to Nurse Sparks.

Nurse Tania Sparks has always been purely professional with her injured soldiers...until sinfully sexy Connor Jordan enters her hospital. He makes her body throb with an intense desire she's never known before. The last thing she wants is to get involved with the injured warrior. So what's a woman supposed to do to relieve her naughty frustrations? Call Kidnap Fantasies and have them supply her with a look-alike man who'll help her forget her sexy soldier...

When Tania and Connor unexpectedly come together at a secluded mountain chalet, their love explodes in a ménage of passion, sensuous desires and a happily forever after.

Contains ménage scenes.

For more Jan Springer stories, please visit
http://www.janspringer.com

_____

Jan's Newsletter

Hi! If you would like to get an email when my books are released, you can sign up here:
Newsletter: http://ymlp.com/xguembmugmgb
Your emails will never be shared and you can unsubscribe whenever you like.

Discover Other Titles by Jan Springer
http://www.janspringer.com

About the Author

Jan Springer writes full-time at her home nestled in cottage country, Ontario, Canada. She enjoys hiking, kayaking, gardening, reading and writing. She is a member of the Writers Union of Canada, Romance Writers of America. She loves hearing from her readers.

A Word From The Author

Hi! Thank you for purchasing this book. Word of mouth is important for any author to succeed. If you enjoyed this story feel free to leave a short review at the place where you bought it. I would really appreciate it. I look forward to bringing you more stories in the near future. Thanks!

If you would like to contact me or personally send me feedback, you can reach me by using my contact page at:

http://janspringerauthor.wordpress.com/contact/

Here are other ways we can connect:
Jan Springer Website at http://www.janspringer.com
Facebook -
https://www.facebook.com/janspringereroticromance
Twitter - https://twitter.com/janspringer @janspringer
Pinterest - http://www.pinterest.com/janspringer1/
Jan's Blog - http://janspringerauthor.wordpress.com/blog-2/
LinkedIn - http://ca.linkedin.com/in/janspringerauthor/
Google Plus -
https://plus.google.com/u/0/101527334949931513035/posts
Jan's Newsletter - http://ymlp.com/xguembmugmgb
Goodreads -
https://www.goodreads.com/author/show/260628.Jan_Springe
r
Happy Reading,
jan springer

Don't miss out!

Click the button below and you can sign up to receive emails whenever Jan Springer publishes a new book. There's no charge and no obligation.

Sign Me Up!

https://books2read.com/r/B-A-WGQ-ULQD

Connecting independent readers to independent writers.

Made in the USA
Middletown, DE
09 April 2024